POWERS UNLEASHED

THE MYSTICAL DIAMOND
Powers Unleashed

THE MYSTICAL DIAMOND
Powers Unleashed

THE MYSTICAL DIAMOND
Powers Unleashed

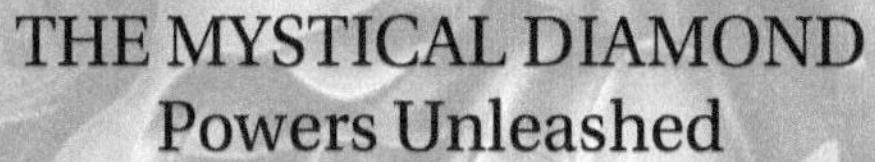

THE MYSTICAL DIAMOND
Powers Unleashed

By Bella Ivy

© Copyright 2021

Cover Design by Cat Cover Design

THE MYSTICAL DIAMOND
Powers Unleashed

Table of Contents

Chapter One
The Letter
10

Chapter Two
Siblings Reunited
22

Chapter Three
The Unexpected Visit
28

Chapter Four
Siblings Divided
46

Chapter Five
Juniper and Darcy Whiteman
54

THE MYSTICAL DIAMOND
Powers Unleashed
Chapter Six
New York City
63

Chapter Seven
The Plan
71

Chapter Eight
Powers Unleashed
79

Chapter Nine
The Diamond Destroyed
94

Chapter Ten
Happily, Ever After
111

Epilogue
Five Years Later
122

THE MYSTICAL DIAMOND
Powers Unleashed

Chapter One
The Letter

20 years later...

It was a calm and starry night. The moon shined bright over the sparking city of Las Vegas, and the trees' branches melodically danced against the roof of a bustling and crowded casino.

Backstage at the arena, Astraea Whiteman clasped the purple velvet cloak at her throat and peered into the glass mirror at her reflection. She cringed at what she saw, finding nothing appealing about the pale, tired face in front of her, empty of a single drop of makeup. Her hair had seen better days, but so had she.

Business was booming, which was great for her wallet, her sense of adventure, and her fancy mansion, but not so good for her need to sleep. She couldn't remember the last time she had a decent night's rest.

But that wasn't the problem.

Not for her, anyway.

Nope, that was never the problem.

With a gentle smile, Astraea concentrated on her face for the longest moment, channeling her energy on all the parts that needed fixing. Then, with a flutter of her fingers, she cast a wave of magic around herself.

Her power burst forth in twinkling swirls of purple smoke. Once the smoke cleared, the woman smiling back at her in the mirror was barely recognizable. She no longer looked like Astraea, the single, thirty-year-old hermit crab who liked to spend her days, when she wasn't on stage, hiding at home in her pajamas, eating copious amounts of junk food, and reading every book she could get her hands on.

Now she looked like Astraea Whiteman, the talented woman everyone came to see tonight. Her long brown hair became sleek and glossy, hanging in thick, perfectly curled locks down her back. Her violet eyes sparkled, emboldened with dark, dramatic makeup, which she didn't have to waste a second on doing herself. Every wrinkle, every sign of exhaustion, was wiped clear from her face, leaving only youthful vibrancy behind.

Astraea was ready, ready to shine!

Just as she was turning away from the mirror, a man wearing a headset and carrying a clipboard popped his head in through the doorway and peeked around the corner at her.

"You're on, Astraea," he said with a smile. He then added, "Oh, by the way, you got a letter. From your sister, Zaina."

Astraea grinned in return as she turned towards him. "Thanks, Fioro. I'll read it after the show. It's probably nothing important anyway."

She was usually not the type to get nervous, but she took a deep breath before starting forward, just to be on the safe side. Like every night, she closed her eyes and held her hand over her chest, sending a silent thanks up to the universe or whoever had given her this strange, but amazing, ability.

"Thank you, Mom and Dad, wherever you both are. I miss you," she whispered.

Having been adopted at a very young age, Astraea never really knew who her true parents were. Her foster parents had been great to her, more than she could ever ask for, but she couldn't help but wonder, from time to time, what could've been if her birth parents never gave them up, never separated them.

She knew she and her siblings were special, too special for the world to handle, but she never thought it would cause so much trouble. As a kid, her powers had been a thing of normalcy, but of fear at the same time. Now it was a source of income and pride, and Astraea was finally ready to let her gift shine.

Opening her eyes, she plastered her stage face on—a cross between a game face and a dazzling, confident smile—and walked out of the dressing room, through the thick black curtains, and onto the stage to greet the roaring cheers of the thousands in the arena waiting to see her.

She waved, smiled, then astounded the audience by sending a shooting bolt of purple sparks out her right hand's palm. The fireworks she started every show with. That was her specialty. The twinkling display set the crowd into an even wilder uproar. They got to their feet, clapping, screaming, already beside themselves, and the first act hadn't even started yet.

But it was about to. And Astraea smirked as she took her position, knowing she was about to blow their minds with a show never seen before.

***

That same evening, far from the Las Vegas Strip where Astraea performed every night as the world's most famous magician, Sage Whiteman walked through the front door of his San Francisco home after a long day on the field at Lightning Stadium.

His wife, Ria, and little girl, Ava, were in the kitchen baking chocolate chip cookies, giggling and laughing as they threw cookie dough at each other. They beamed at him when he walked in, sweaty from the hours of exertion behind him.

"How was work?" Ria asked as he strolled into their midst and gave them both a light peck on the cheek.

"Great." Sage smiled, his face as vibrant and youthful as it had been fifteen years ago when he was only a young, sporty teenager. He always managed to stay energized by using his ability—which was why he was known as the greatest football coach and former player in all of history.

The San Francisco Flares had been continuous winners in his early college years, back when he was the star player, the best ever seen in football history. But their winning streak never ended because immediately after Sage quit the team as a player, he joined it as their head coach. With his super speed, strength, and passion for sports, it was impossible for him *not* to be a fabulous coach. His enthusiasm was contagious, and he made the others strive to do their best too.

However, no one, of course, knew the truth about Sage's flawless physical abilities. They just assumed he was one of the lucky ones who were excellent at sports, never got tired, and never ran out of energy. And they were right—or at least half right. He wanted to let them know, let someone know, many times, but he always feared that once he did, his career would be over, forever branded as a cheater.

"I'm just so excited for the upcoming game," he added. "It's going to be the greatest one of the season. I can already tell. How was your day? Did this little devil act up again?" Sage teased as he leaned down and pinched his daughter's face.

"Wonderful," Ria said. "I sold two houses today, and Ava made it onto the honor roll at school."

"Yes!" Sage punched the air with an impassioned fist, then reached across the kitchen counter to sneak a finger into the bowl of cookie dough.

When his daughter began to pout, he moved his hand, veering instead towards her, tickling her stomach and grinning at the shrill giggles rising out of her.

"Oh, by the way, Sage," Ria said, once Ava's laughter had ceased, "you got a letter in the mail today. From your sister, Zaina."

"Zaina?" Sage shrugged. "Cool. I'll read it in a little bit—I need to shower first. Be back in a second, ladies."

And when he said *be back in a second,* he wasn't kidding.

The moment Sage flung a leg out, his powers kicked in, affording him a speed that even the fastest animals in the world could never keep up with. He was nothing but a blur, flying into his bedroom, zooming into the shower.

The water turned on, then turned off thirty seconds later. Wet and thoroughly clean, Sage stepped out, finished with the whole operation that took no more than two minutes.

He grinned at his reflection in the mirror, then headed out to join his family once again.

***

Across the country, Cristiano clicked off the lamp at his desk, and then rose with a sigh as he stretched out his taut body.

At this hour, the building wasn't empty, but most of its workers had gone home for the night. That was the trouble with Cristiano—he could never seem to turn off his workaholic tendencies. He was constantly thinking about terrorism, assassinations, and other threats to the country.

It was nearly midnight, but his brain was wired. It would be awhile before he could relax enough to sleep—if he was able to sleep at all.

Swooping up the jacket draped over his chair, he slipped it on, then headed out of the FBI headquarters and started for his apartment complex on the outskirts of Washington, D.C. The night was dark and quiet, as it often was at this time. Cristiano loved it—he loved the darkness. He felt comfortable being unseen.

But that wasn't just a recent development, a new tendency born out of his complicated work days. Cristiano had always been that way.

He thought, randomly, of his childhood as he crossed the empty street. Back then, his desire to be invisible had manifested in his young-minded decision to run away from the orphanage and live in a library. A library was a great place to be unseen. There were always more shelves to hide behind, more books to blend in with. He was allowed to be silent there, silent and shadowy. Just as he was now in his job. His childhood tendency had become an ability, and now, it had become his lifestyle.

Good thing, too, because Cristiano had never been good at most jobs. He'd encountered a lot of them in his early twenties. A department store clerk, a waiter, a car salesman, he'd done them all. But those jobs didn't suit him. They were too... *visible.*

So, he decided to reach out to the FBI, and once they were told of his secret abilities, they hired him on the spot. It was a risk, for sure, but he knew that he would be too much of a valuable asset for them to lock him up. He didn't even need to complete his application.

After all, what was more valuable to the nation's security than a man who could become invisible at will and see the future? He could stop any terrorist plan in their tracks, even before they got started. He was a priceless strength to the government.

But now... he was starting to think he didn't want to be unseen anymore. He had grown tired of sneaking around, not being able to tell anyone about his job and what he did. He had even lost friends as a result of his secrecy.

With a heavy sigh, he reached his apartment building. He went up the elevator, entered the code on the keypad, and then stepped into the empty home.

Cristiano's shoes touched something slippery on the floor. Frowning, he looked down and saw the pile of envelopes that the mailman had shoved through the slot in his door. He sighed and reached for the pile, then began sifting through it on the spot.

"Bills, bills, bills, and more bills. When will these ever end?" he murmured to himself as he tossed several of them onto the already piled stack he had waiting for him, taunting him.

Cristiano usually wasn't the kind of guy who could let mail sit unopened for hours. He was the type to rip the bandage off sooner than later. But he had been too distracted lately to deal with his life's responsibilities.

Most of the mail was what he had expected. But there was one envelope that stood out. It looked different from the others—not as long and skinny as the classic bill envelope. It was bright pink with stars and glitter on it, a classic signature of someone very close to him. Plus, his sister's name was on the return address.

"A letter from Zaina?" Cristiano smiled to himself. He'd always been fond of Zaina—she was a quiet one, like himself.

His other sister, Astraea, while part of the family that he loved, had always been too boisterous for his taste. But Zaina... Zaina was a kindred spirit. And she didn't write often. What was she up to? It had been years since they last saw each other.

Stepping further into his apartment, Cristiano dropped the coupons on the kitchen counter and then drifted into the living room. Living in the country's capital was not cheap by any means. If it wasn't for his coupons, he might have never made it through his first year.

His favorite recliner chair sat waiting for him in front of the TV, all soft and plush and upholstered in purple velvet. That was where he always crashed to wind down with a lighthearted show and something sugary—*when* he had the time, of course.

He sat down, popped open a can of soda, and opened Zaina's letter.

***

At the exact same moment, in Las Vegas and San Francisco, the other two siblings, Astraea and Sage, sat down to open their letters too.

Despite not having spoken to each other in ages, the quintuplets were still connected in astonishing ways, their synchronization being one of them. Three of the five opened their letter from Zaina at the same time, in the same way, and began reading.

Hey, it's Zaina.

Hope you're doing well.

Things are going good here, but I miss my family. It's been a while!

Would you like to join Theo, Bord, and me for a Christmas get-together?

I know you're probably busy, but we all would really like to see you again.

I'm planning for Saturday, the nineteenth. Two o'clock.

Hope you can make it.

-Z.

Chapter Two
Siblings Reunited

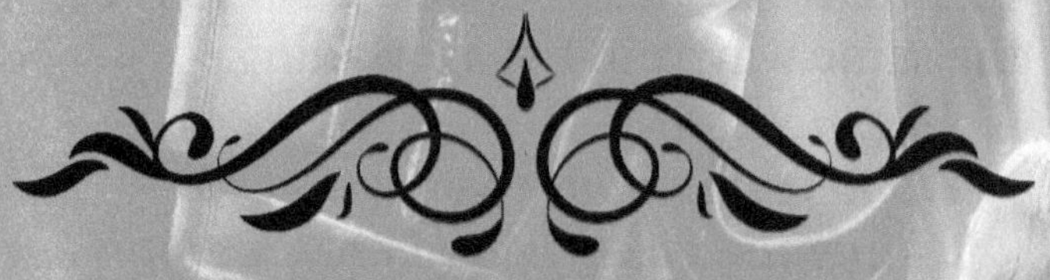

Astraea stepped off the plane and cringed. Winters in New Hampshire were much more brutal than they were in Nevada. Just a few hours ago, she'd been in hot, sunny, desert weather. Now she was surrounded by trees, snow, and people bundled up in a million layers. She herself had forgotten about the temperature change and had neglected to bolster her sparse t-shirt and shorts ensemble.

She stood shivering, arms wrapped around her middle, as she searched the faces out front for her sister's. It had been years since they last saw each other, and for a minute, Astraea wondered if she'd even recognize Zaina. It didn't take long for Astraea to realize that they all looked the same.

Finally, she spotted her hurrying towards her from the parking lot's west end, her long black hair tied in a messy knot on the top of her head. She was running so fast; it almost looked like she was flying. Like most people around here, she was decked out in at least three layers of clothing, including a bulky wool coat. She carried another one in her free hand as if she dared to wear two at one time.

When she saw Astraea, her pale face broke out into a smile. All the siblings were the same age, but Zaina Whiteman looked younger for some reason, probably since she was the baby in the family and always will be. Her smooth skin rarely needed a drop of makeup, and her purple eyes were always bright with youth and vibrancy. She looked twenty, not thirty. Astraea smiled back as she hurried towards her.

The sisters shared a brief embrace that warmed Astraea up from the inside out. And when they pulled away, Zaina passed her the wool coat with a smile.

"I thought you might need this."

Astraea grinned and fitted her arms through the sleeves. She still felt like she was going to freeze to death, but at least the biting edge had disappeared from the chilly air.

Folding her arms around her middle, she cast a glance around the airport's parking lot and asked Zaina, "Thanks, you're a lifesaver. Where are the others?"

Zaina shrugged, then frowned. "Hey, how did you know I invited the others?"

Astraea rolled her eyes with a playful chuckle and tapped the center of her forehead. "Mind reader, remember? Besides, that's totally something you would do. You've always been big on family."

Zaina's cheeks flushed. "I hope you're not mad."

With a snort, Astraea shook her head. "Not at all. Heck, I'm excited. It's been at least a couple years since I last saw those pesky brothers of mine! I bet they're all old and fat." She chuckled to herself, but Zaina didn't return the smile. Her face clouded over like fog that was rolling in to chase the sun.

"I just wish... Alaric..." She didn't finish her sentence, but she didn't have to. Astraea nodded with understanding, dropping her expression to a somber one.

But almost a second later, the two sisters were smiling again.

They'd spotted Sage, their favorite brother, emerging from the sliding airport doors with his wife and daughter in tow.

"Hey, sisters!" Sage called, raising his voice so loud that several people nearby shot him concerning glances.

To the amusement of his family, he broke out into a run, showing off his supernatural speed. To Zaina and Astraea, he looked like a blur zooming towards them. To the other people in the vicinity, Sage wasn't visible at all. He completely disappeared from the atmosphere until, a second later, he was standing directly in front of his siblings.

Behind him, his wife and daughter marched forward to join him.

"So, Sage, what brings you here?" Astraea asked, teasingly.

"Oh, you know—Christmas, family, the prospect of a *delicious* meal."

Zaina chuckled. "You're in luck. Theo is at home cooking it now." Zaina herself wasn't skilled at cooking, but her husband, a professional private chef, always kept their whole family well-fed with delicious dishes.

Sometimes she'd think the food was the only reason her siblings kept coming back.

The next few minutes were spent mingling with each other and passing around hugs and smiles. After greeting Sage's wife, both Zaina and Astraea bent down to say hi to the little blond-haired girl clinging to her mother's side. Ava's face broke out into a smile when both her aunts handed out chocolates and caramels.

And by the time they straightened up, the last member of their gathering was striding towards them.

Cristiano hadn't bothered dressing down for this get-together. He looked a bit like a Secret Service guard striding towards them, suit pressed and crisp, tinted glasses black and opaque, poker face the best they'd ever seen. At the sight of him, Ava tensed and clung to her mother's leg, tears welling in her eyes.

Even the adults at the scene were intimidated by Cristiano. The siblings almost didn't recognize him as their brother until he paused in front of them and took off his sunglasses to reveal his deep green eyes.

"Oh," he said, looking around the group. "I see this is a... multi-person event."

Astraea snorted and rolled her eyes. "Duh! Do you think our sweet little Zaina would be so exclusive to only invite one of us to her holiday party?"

With that, she tossed her arms around Cristiano's middle (he was way too tall for her to reach his neck), but he stiffened immediately and broke contact.

Stoic though he was, everyone loved Cristiano. Like all the quintuplets, there was a magnetic aura attached to each of them. It came with the supernatural territory, an extra quirk in association with their various psychic powers. So, within seconds, their intimidation was forgotten.

Everyone in the group was smiling, slapping him on the back, and giving him one-armed hugs since he hated physical contact.

And so, having all gathered, they piled into Zaina's SUV and headed north.

Nobody mentioned the fifth sibling.

But all four of them thought about his name.

Chapter Three
The Unexpected Visit

"Well, here we are! Our humble abode!"

Zaina parked in front of the big, rambling log cabin and cut the engine with a smile. She turned to look at everyone in the backseat and added, "Isn't it great?"

Alighted from the car, the whole crew took a minute to stare up at the structure in front of them.

Zaina loved being in nature, so the cabin in the woods was a dream come true for her. It was set at the end of a long dirt road, winding between a dense forest like a slithering snake. The logs were stained a glossy chestnut-brown, and the house boasted a wide, wraparound porch that Zaina loved to sit on and drink her coffee every morning.

Astraea cringed at the biting cold again and tried to bat away a mosquito buzzing around her head. "It's... nice." She was the city girl of their family—no surprise since she performed every night on the Las Vegas Strip.

Living a solitary life would drive her insane. No bars, no restaurants, no theaters? It was her worst nightmare.

Cristiano, who also enjoyed the city life and his tiny apartment in the heart of it, grimaced at the twigs and dirt on the ground. Without bothering to mask his true feelings, he said, "Yes. It's nice."

But Sage was a bit more enthusiastic about it. He saw the woods around him as a challenge. "Wow! Think of all the running I could do here—all the trees I could climb up! No longer will I have pesky neighbors yelling at me in the middle of the night to stop being noisy. If it wasn't for my coaching job, I'd run away from San Fran and get a cabin in the woods just like this. Wouldn't that be nice, Ria?"

His wife chuckled nervously. She was clearly not a fan of the cabin either.

Looking around at everything with the wide-eyed wonder of a curious child, Ava wrinkled her nose at the savory scent in the air and asked, "What's that smell?"

Zaina smiled at her niece. "Theo's food. Let's go see what he's cooking up for us."

The lot of them resembled a small army as they stalked toward the house and ambled up its creaky front steps. The delicious smells were strong here on the front porch, but they didn't really hit them until Zaina threw open the door and let them all inside.

All at once, everyone's stomachs began growling. Nobody even realized how hungry they were until they were inside Zaina's house.

"Wow!" Sage exclaimed. "Whatever that is, give me a heaping helping of it!"

Chuckles traveled through their group, and then Zaina instructed everyone to get comfortable. Astraea immediately kicked off her shoes, shrugged off her jacket, and dropped them into the foyer's corner without a care in the world. Sage showed the same boldness as he flung his coat off, but his wife and daughter were far more polite.

Only Cristiano remained as stiff as ever—he didn't even bother to remove his suit jacket. All he did was drop his sunglasses into his pocket and then look around in a questioning manner.

"Do you have a library?" he finally asked.

Zaina's mouth turned up at the corners. "Sure do. You know I can't live without my books. Down the hall, the second door on the left. But don't you want to eat first?"

"Food? Oh, right. Sure."

The entire ground level had an open floor plan, so it only took Zaina a few steps to lead her family into the kitchen up ahead. There, they all met Theo, who was babysitting a steaming pot of something, and young eight-year-old Bord, who was helping his dad in the ways he could; stirring a bowl, sprinkling seasonings, gathering ingredients out of the fridge and pantry.

Together, the two of them had created a huge holiday feast, complete with five to six desserts, two hams, and an array of delicious side dishes and appetizers that spanned the entire dining room table.

After greeting each other and passing around more hugs, the whole family sat down at the table before mounds of savory-smelling food. Wine bottles were brought out and opened, and then the party began. But it was no ordinary Christmas party. How could it be when half of the family was clairvoyant?

Zaina, for example, kept using her telekinetic powers to bring food towards her. Instead of asking one of the others to pass the salad, she focused her psychic energy on the salad bowl. She sent it levitating in the air, where it floated before she slowly guided it back down towards her. It was a sight to see and made Ava, the niece who hadn't witnessed her aunt's ability too often, gasp with wonder.

"Wow! The salad is flying!" she exclaimed in excitement.

Astraea used her mind-reading ability to analyze the thoughts around her and figure out when someone was about to snag the last roll of bread or piece of pie so she could get it for herself first. But Sage, who was equally crafty, took advantage of his inhumanly fast speed to thwart Astraea before she even had a chance to reach across the table.

Cristiano was the only one who didn't use his ability. Though he would have preferred to tap into his invisibility, disappear from the table for a while, and come back after he'd spent an hour or two in Zaina's library with a good book, he stayed at the table.

Even though he typically chose to be alone over company, he really had missed his family, and the food was impeccable, some of the best he had in years.

Of course, his neglect to use his power meant he wasn't tuned into the future like he usually was. He used to be so focused, his instincts so aware of any potential danger coming their way. So, naturally, he didn't see what was about to happen to all of them.

After dinner, the family abandoned the mess in the kitchen and dining room and headed into the living room. The fireplace flickered from across the room, warming up the couches and recliner chairs positioned all around the inviting space. Here, they gathered with plates of dessert and glasses of wine.

Everyone was becoming drowsy, relaxing into their chairs and sugar comas. It was the best part of the day, the calmest.

Well, only for a few minutes.

The movie playing on the big flat-screen had barely gotten through the opening credits when a flash of light appeared through the uncovered windows, turning the whole outside world, briefly, into a bright blue light show.

And when the lights faded, a man stood there in its place, as if he'd been shot out of the lights like a firework explosion.

The man was the fifth quintuplet, the one nobody had invited.

"Alaric," Zaina gasped.

Astraea stood up so fast that she nearly knocked over the end table beside her chair. "You didn't invite him, did you?"

Zaina had tears in her eyes. Shaking her head, she cried, "No! Of course not."

Theo rushed to her side like a bodyguard, shielding her with his arms as they curled around her shoulders. "Don't worry," he murmured.

But Zaina continued to shake her head. "You don't understand. You don't... you don't *know* him."

And if there was anyone who knew Alaric, it was Zaina. She knew him even more than the other siblings. They only knew their brother was evil and hell-bent on causing as many ruckuses as he could in life. They didn't know the extent of his evilness, or how powerful he truly was, or all the other things Zaina had learned during her brief stint on his side.

She tried not to think about those times... she had been only ten years old after all. She hadn't known any better. But that didn't stop the memories, which stained her mind and refused to be cleared away.

"Maybe... maybe he's changed?" Sage, always the one with a positive outlook on everything in life, proposed this idea. But nobody even glanced sideways at him, let alone gave his nonsensical idea any attention.

They knew better than that. Alaric had always been Alaric, and he always would be Alaric.

Evil.

Their best bet now would be to band together, to keep their family safe from him. There was no doubt in their minds that he was still the same selfish and greedy brother they had known decades ago.

That is, if he meant them harm. But did he? No one had stopped to think about why he was there in the first place.

But Astraea did. Furrowing her brow at the sight of her brother outside, shaking an autumn leaf off the hem of his jeans in contempt, she asked the others, "What do you think he wants? I mean, if he wanted to kill us, he's powerful enough to explode the whole house or something. He could do it in a heartbeat."

"There must be another reason," Cristiano agreed solemnly.

With a sharp edge to her voice, Zaina asked, "Well, can we please go meet him outside? I don't want that man in this house."

"Good idea." Sage nodded, then turned to his wife. "Honey, do you mind staying in here? Keep an eye on Ava."

"Yes, you too, Theo," Zaina added, throwing worried glances at her husband and son.

Four of the quints rose with the fluidity of one person. Moving in a single-file line, they marched to the front door, Sage at the head of their group, Zaina at the very back.

Swirling December winds hit them in the face as the door was flung open. Together, they spilled out of the house and into the yard, where they faced Alaric, four to one.

Alaric smiled at his siblings with the air of a wolf smiling down at small, helpless woodland creatures.

"Good afternoon, brothers and sisters. Celebrating Christmas without me? I'm hurt."

His deep red eyes flashed, roaming down the line and stopping on each of their faces for one chilling moment.

Sage took charge of the situation with two forward steps. "Listen, Alaric. You're family, and we love you, but unless you've had a change of heart in the last twenty years, you're not welcome here."

Alaric raised an eyebrow. "Change of heart? What do you mean, exactly? I mean, I suppose you could say I had a change of heart this morning. I planned to have cereal for breakfast and then, at the last minute, changed my mind and had pancakes instead."

Astraea snarled. "Nope. He hasn't changed. He's as maddening as always."

Alaric's eyes flitted in her direction. "Astraea! Beautiful, talented Astraea. You know, just last night, I was watching you on TV, performing one of your many shows in Vegas. Impressive. I bet no one suspects the magic you do is *real*."

Looking back at Sage now, Alaric continued, "And you! You're doing an awesome job yourself. Congrats on leading your team to victory."

He went on to praise Cristiano's new stoic attitude and Zaina's lovely home and family, making all of them frown in confusion.

"How do you even know all that stuff about us?" Astraea asked. "We thought you were trapped in that cave."

Alaric chuckled. "That was twenty years ago, sis. The cave and I had a good run, but I missed the freedom of the outside—most of all, I missed you guys. So, I escaped. I've been keeping tabs on you all for a while now."

All the siblings' faces clouded over, dimness stealing the remains of light left in their eyes. If Alaric had escaped, that meant he must've been even more powerful than he was when they trapped him.

That kind of power was the kind that needed to stay buried—what would happen to them, what would happen to the *world,* now that those powers had been set free?

What were his reasons for keeping track of the other quints?

Cristiano voiced this very question just as the others were thinking about it. "What's up with the constant surveillance?" he asked in his cool, monotonous voice, the one he reserved for his investigative work.

Alaric batted at a leaf that had fallen onto his wavy black head with a grunt of disgust. As he caught it, he crushed it in his fist, then viciously scattered the brown and orange flakes all over the ground.

"I'll tell you why," he said. "Because I'm tired of doing everything alone. I need backup. I need *you* guys. So, join me. Alone, I'm, well, pretty dang invincible. But if the five of us banded together, we could all be twenty times more invincible."

"Band together to do what, Alaric?" Zaina asked. "Unless your plans are actually normal, like, having weekend family cookouts together or the five of us and our families going on a cruise, I don't think any of us will be interested in what you have to offer."

Alaric's eyes took on a new look as they surveyed Zaina. Their history had been, and would probably always be, a barrier of contention between them. Zaina hated Alaric for influencing her as a child, and she hated herself even more for falling for it.

Alaric hated Zaina, likewise, for betraying him just when he thought he'd found a lifelong partner. With equal animosity, the two glared at each other, their stares so heated they almost fired up the cold air around them.

Then Alaric said, "Not even... taking over this world and starting a new one?" He addressed the others now, red eyes scanning each of their faces. "I know you all have problems with society, just like I do. The world hasn't treated us kindly. Sure, we all have excellent careers, but... beyond that?

Astraea, people love you when you get on stage and perform "magic tricks," but how do you think they'd view you if you came out as a *real* magician? They'd probably call you a demon-possessed freak!

And Sage, what about the sports industry that tossed you aside just because you reached a certain age? You're the best player the world ever had, but you're shoved off to the side to be a coach instead of on the field where you should be.

Cristiano, aren't you tired of lying to those around you all the time? I know what you do for a living. It's not really that much of a secret. Don't you want a life where you don't have to stay invisible?

And Zaina, I know you live a pretty cushioned life already—but what about your son? Don't you want guaranteed happiness for him for the rest of his life? This world is going to hell, and we all know it. So why not do something about it before it destroys us?"

The four siblings frowned at Alaric. Inside the private confines of their minds, they were all thinking a myriad of different thoughts.

Sage was thinking, *Sure, it'd be nice if society didn't cast away the old guys as much, but it's not that big of a deal. I enjoy being a coach.*

Zaina was thinking, *I don't need a fortune to give Bord a good life. He'll have a good life because he's loved. That's enough for me.*

Cristiano thought, *Joke's on him. I actually like being unseen. It suits me.*

But Astraea was thinking, *Huh. He's evil, but he's got a point. Everyone worships me, but they don't even know the real me. They'd probably throw salt and holy water on me the minute they found out the truth. Maybe even cart me off to be experimented on. People can be so cruel and judgmental. Why couldn't they just accept me for who I am? Alaric's right... this world needs a new way of thinking... an attitude adjustment, that's all.*

"There's no way I'll agree to join you," Zaina spat.

The others nodded and offered the same sentiment.

But Astraea, tilting her head inquiringly, asked, "How would you even take over the world and change it or whatever? I mean, you're powerful, but not that powerful."

"I have my ways, Astraea." Alaric smirked. "Why? Are you considering it?"

Zaina, Cristiano, and Sage whipped their heads in her direction and fixed her with fiery glares, daring her to give Alaric an answer.

"Astraea, you're not—?" Zaina pleaded with her sister, but she couldn't bring herself to finish the question.

Astraea shrugged. "I... I'm not. I'm just asking. Why is that so bad? I mean, how do we even know his plans are evil? Maybe he's got a pretty laidback plan in mind."

Zaina raised an eyebrow, glaring at her sister, her sister who had always been so logical and reasonable, with an unmasked scorn. "This is Alaric we're talking about. He *lives* for evilness and destruction. You know that, Astraea."

But did she? She may just be naïve, but she couldn't help but think that, perhaps, Alaric had changed in the twenty years since they'd last met. After all, ten-year-olds, especially those with endless power at their fingertips, couldn't be expected to make wise decisions.

Clearly, Alaric was still hooked on the take-over-the-world mindset, but maybe he would do it better this time. Maybe he wouldn't be so destructive.

"Astraea?" Zaina prompted, lifting both eyebrows now. With that one look and that one utterance of her name, she conveyed all the shock and worry she felt at her sister's delayed response. Surely Astraea wasn't considering...?

But then again, Astraea had become the most self-centered of all of us. She used to be so giving and kind, always looking out for others, but the fame had really gotten into her head. She lives in the spotlight. Everyone praising her all the time. Plus, her magic...

Astraea heard her sister's thoughts, but she ignored them. Instead, she tuned into Alaric's headspace, searching his thoughts for anything malicious. But his mind was strangely blank. All she heard was his voice speaking directly to her.

Hello, Astraea. I know you're in here. Are you considering joining me?

Maybe, Astraea replied. *But I have to know your heart's in the right place. Show me what you're really thinking.*

Of course. But first... let me show you this image...

Alaric filled his thoughts with one resounding picture, the image so strong that it took over his entire head and Astraea's as well. It was the image of the purple diamond, the same purple diamond from twenty years before, dangling from a necklace chain. As it swayed back and forth, Astraea couldn't help but follow the motions with her mind's eye.

Back and forth, back and forth.

The diamond swayed, glowing with an inner light that swept like sun rays throughout both Alaric and Astraea's brains. She thought they destroyed the diamond, took all its powers, and left it useless. Now it was back, bigger and more powerful than before.

And then Astraea heard his voice, echoing in her mind as if it was her own. *You will join me, Astraea. You will use your powers to stop the others, and you will join me on my journey.*

Yes, she responded.

Alaric took the diamond out of her thoughts, and at once, she was released from the mental connection. But the veil that blanketed her mind, enchanting her, remained. A strong urge pulsed through her, as intense as the fog clouding her thoughts.

Out of nowhere, she whirled on her siblings and flung the full force of her magic on them before they even realized what had happened. Jets of purple smoke left her fingertips in swirls and curlicues that swept through the air and enveloped her brothers and sister. It happened in the blink of an eye—as soon as the smoke touched them, all three of them were frozen in place, paralyzed.

Astraea smiled and turned to Alaric. "Now they can't stop us."

With a wide smile of his own, Alaric nodded appreciatively at his sister.

"Excellent, Astraea. Your powers are impressive. Combined with mine, we'll be unstoppable. Now come on—let's get out of this dump. We have a world to take over."

Chapter Four
Siblings Divided

Zaina, Cristiano, and Sage felt nothing, only emptiness. There wasn't any pain, not even any numbness, just a strange nothingness. An absence of a heartbeat or of steady breaths. Non-blinking eyes and skin that didn't register the chill in the air. And, of course, limbs that wouldn't move.

However, their brains were still in motion. Astraea had only frozen their bodies, but their minds whizzed with a zillion thoughts, each one more panicky than the last.

Sage was thinking, *Dang. It's like we're ten years old all over again. Except I never expected Astraea to turn on us. She was always the good one, the sensible one. Figured it would be Zaina.*

Zaina was thinking, *I can't believe her. What are we going to do? Her powers are greater than ours—how will we stop her?*

And Cristiano, immediately shifting into the FBI agent mode he rarely left behind, thought, *Okay, there's got to be a way to track him. If only he had a cell phone or a laptop...*

But their thoughts were abruptly cut off as their senses restarted. As soon as Astraea and Alaric left—using Astraea's magic to conjure a portal—the spell Astraea put on the siblings was severed. Its energy fizzled, bringing life and movement back to everyone's bodies.

As the three quints were adjusting to their newly unfrozen state, Sage took charge of the situation like the responsible and compassionate big brother he'd always been.

"Guys, let's head inside," he said. "It won't do us any good to freeze to death out here. So, let's just sit down for a minute, get our bearings. Then we can figure out what to do next."

In silence, Zaina and Cristiano nodded, then turned to follow Sage.

Things were tense for the next half hour inside the cabin. It was a strange contrast—the tension and fear in the midst of the cozy flickering fireplace and the warm smells of Christmas dinner, which, by now, had gotten cold.

Not wanting to worry the children, Zaina sent her son, Bord, into his bedroom and asked him to entertain his cousin Ava. Once the two were gone, everyone gathered in the living room to discuss the situation that had just happened.

"Alaric has always been big-minded," Zaina reminded her siblings from her place on the couch, nestled into Theo's side. "I remember that from when we were younger. Even way back then, the plans he had in mind had been huge. I don't doubt he'll have big plans now too."

"I'd assume you're right. I mean, taking over the world is no small feat." Sage meant for his comment to be a joke, a mood-lightener, but nobody laughed. Instead, everyone stared grimly at him, their eyes dark with worry.

"I just don't even know where to start," Zaina murmured.

"Alright, let's think about this." Sage sighed and leaned towards the others, resting his arms on his knees with his usual pep-talk-giving, football coach demeanor. "Astraea has magic and can read minds, right?"

Cristiano and Zaina gave solemn nods in response.

Sage continued, "Right. *But* I'm pretty sure she has to be close to the person she's spying on to read their thoughts. So, since she won't be able to hear us, she won't know what we're planning. So that's good, right?"

"But what *are* we planning?" Zaina asked with innocent curiosity.

For a moment, Sage seemed at a loss for words. The orange flames from the fireplace cast shadows on his anxious expression, emphasizing his downcast eyes and the taut line of his mouth.

But then his gaze shifted to his brother, who sat stoically in the armchair, unmoving.

"What do you think, Cristiano?" Sage asked. "You deal with terrorists and criminals in your line of work all the time. What do you think we should do?"

To everyone's surprise, Cristiano, who was usually in a constant state of silence, sat forward and belted out a long speech.

"Honestly," he said, "Alaric is not that powerful. He can control the elements, and he has a part of the diamond, which enhances his abilities, of course. If he *wanted* to, he could use his power to conjure an explosion or an earthquake or something.

But I don't think he wants to destroy the world—it sounds like he wants to *mold* it. To change it, so everyone worships him. But to do that, he'll need Astraea. She's the only one with the magic and the power to read minds—she's his greatest asset."

"So, what, we just need to take Astraea away from him?"

Cristiano nodded at Zaina. "That's the first step, anyway. But we can't just thwart his plans. That's not enough. The only way we can be totally safe is to change his mind completely. We need to convince him that he'd be better off changing his ways. Perhaps the answer is to appeal to his sense of humanity, to the things that brought him happiness as a child, and remind him that we're family. If we can restore that hope for him, maybe he'll turn good."

"How is that possible?" Sage asked. "Alaric had a horrible childhood. First, he was adopted into an abusive family, remember? Then he was raised by wolves, literally, when he ran away to live in the woods. Does he even have *any* good memories?"

This was an eye-opening reminder that everyone agreed with. Sage was right. From the time he was a baby, Alaric had been surrounded by darkness. He certainly hadn't gotten a promising start to his life, so why should they expect him to have any hope now?

But... there might have been *something.*

Slowly, Zaina rose from the couch, her eyes unfocused, hovering on the hearthrug in front of the fire but seeing something else entirely.

"Zaina, honey, what's wrong?" Theo asked.

She said lowly as if musing her own thoughts aloud, "Alaric's never had any hope, but he's always had... dreams. And those dreams shaped every decision he ever made. He never *wanted* to be evil. He only wanted... family."

Sage frowned. Cristiano's eyebrows twitched slightly, but his face stayed a blank page.

"What do you mean?"

Her eyes came back into focus. She stepped out of her own memory and faced the others, a new, wild light in her gaze. "Guys, I just remembered! When Alaric and I were together, he had this treehouse in the woods—he called it his command center. And the place was *full* of newspaper clippings and magazine articles and all sorts of stuff.

All of it was centered around family. Pictures of parents with little kids his age. All he ever wanted was to find our birth parents and see if they would give him the love he craved. That's what made him the person he is today—that void that came about when he realized he had parents somewhere out there that he'd never met."

"That's it!" Then, like a rocket, Sage jolted up out of his chair, slamming his palms together in a clap. "If we can just find our birth parents and have them reunite with Alaric, we could change everything."

"We also need to get the diamond away from him," Cristiano added. "That thing enhances *everything,* including negative feelings. It'll be fueling his evil desires."

"Right." Zaina nodded, took a deep breath, then said, "So basically, the cure to our problems is to get Astraea back on our side, find our birth parents whom we've never met in our life, and steal a diamond that Alaric never lets out of his sight?"

Sage shrugged. "Yeah, that's about right."

The weight of the situation nearly suffocated them. They sat in silence for a long moment, processing the intensity of everything they had to do.

Then, thankfully, Theo spoke up with a strong proposal, a good first step to the harrowing journey ahead of them.

"How about a pot of coffee?" he offered.

Chapter Five
Juniper and Darcy Whiteman

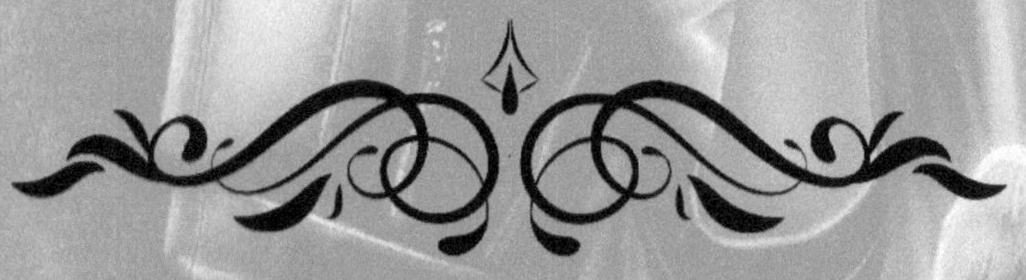

After the coffee had been brewed and passed around, along with some delicious brownie cake, the plan was decided, and roles were dished out.

Cristiano would be in charge of scouring the Internet. He would use his investigation skills to help with the search for their birth parents. Zaina and Sage would be on Astraea duty—they would try their best, first and foremost, to find their sister, then to convince her to come back to the side of good.

Cristiano was also put in charge of the purple diamond. His invisibility power was the one thing that could allow them to get close enough to Alaric to take the diamond. But, of course, his role wouldn't come into play until they actually *found* Alaric.

Finding Alaric was also partly Cristiano's job. His theory was simple. Alaric wouldn't be easily traceable in ordinary circumstances because he was always living in the woods.

But now that he was planning on manipulating millions of people, he would need to be out in the open, somewhere where a lot of people could fall under his influence.

So, Cristiano's plan was to hack into the surveillance systems of all the places where a multitude might be reached: the capitol, TV stations, airports, city centers.

And after a while, his plan worked. He found out that Alaric Whiteman had bought two one-way plane tickets for New York City that was leaving that evening. More digging brought another interesting fact to light.

There was a huge Christmas event happening in Central Park tomorrow afternoon. Cristiano couldn't be sure, but he had a creeping suspicion that Alaric was planning to begin his take-over-the-world speech at the event. And with Astraea's magic involved... the two of them could hypnotize *millions* of people.

"Cristiano! Cristiano!" Zaina came running into the office like a caffeinated cheetah, her face alight with a bright-eyed smile. She was waving a piece of paper in her hand.

When Cristiano looked up from the computer to question her about it, she announced, "I found my birth certificate! It was in a box with all my stuff from my parents' house—they must have gotten it from the orphanage—anyway, *look*!"

In a flurry of excitement, Zaina dropped the certificate down on the desk, covering the keyboard. Cristiano peered down at the official paper, and his eyes immediately found the names *Juniper and Darcy Whiteman.* Their parents.

"Awesome, Zaina." Cristiano nodded in approval. "Now that we've got their names, I should be able to find them easily."

"What about Alaric and Astraea?" Zaina wrung her hands together. She was a ball of nerves, practically flying up and down with anxious energy.

As calm as always, Cristiano explained his findings in a clear, cool voice while he typed furiously at the keyboard.

"Wow. New York." Zaina slumped against the desk and heaved a sigh. "That's really far. And expensive. But we have to do it, don't we?"

"Yes. I've already booked our plane tickets."

Zaina's eyes widened. "A-All of us?"

"Yes. Well, not all of us. I'm saving a little money on myself—being invisible and all. I won't need a ticket. We'll be leaving tonight."

"That only gives us a few hours to find Juniper and Darcy." A frantic note entered Zaina's voice, lifting her cadence towards a girlish, high-pitched squeal.

"A few hours?" Cristiano snorted, a rare glimpse of mirth filling his usually blank face. "I've already found them."

Zaina gasped. She glued her eyes to the screen where Cristiano's skill and speed had worked wonders. Using the hacking techniques essential to his FBI work, it took him no time at all to find his birth mother and father. Juniper and Darcy Whiteman lived in the suburbs of Syracuse.

"Syracuse!" Zaina practically screamed the word. "That's in New York!"

"Yes, it is, Zaina." Cristiano smiled a real full-blown smile. "They're not that far from where we'll be, in Central Park."

Sage dashed into the room so fast he was barely a blur. "I heard screaming. What happened?"

Zaina and Cristiano filled him in on everything that had transpired in the last few minutes. Sage had a giant grin on his face by the end of the story.

"Hey, right on!" he shouted. "That means we're as good as done, doesn't it?"

"Not quite..." Cristiano turned away from the computer and slowly lifted his eyes toward his siblings. "Finding our parents is just half the problem. Now we have to find out if they actually *want* to meet us. If we just show up, they might not recognize us and call the cops. I can't have that on my record."

That wiped the smile off Sage's face in a heartbeat. Zaina's mouth drew down into a frown, her eyes glistening with tears.

"Is there a phone number?" she asked. Already her voice sounded strained as if she was on the verge of sobbing.

Cristiano nodded somberly and scrawled the digits on a scrap piece of paper. Zaina reached for it, then pulled her cell phone out of her pocket.

Looking at each of her brothers, she said, "I'll be right back," and then disappeared into the next room.

Zaina bit her bottom lip and listened to the phone ring. By the second ring, she was tapping her toe on the floor and staring unblinkingly out the living room window, at the spot where Alaric had just stood a cluster of minutes ago. Her heartbeat raced, and by the time the third ring happened, she was sweating.

On the fourth ring, there was a click, and a soft, feminine voice answered, "Hello?"

She didn't sound like an old woman, though knowing what her adoptive parents had told her about her birth parents, she knew that Juniper and Darcy were in their early twenties when the quints were born—which would make them well into their fifties now.

But the woman who answered sounded no older than Zaina herself, with a light, airy voice that brought images of sea breezes and wind chimes to Zaina's mind.

She smiled to herself, then blinked past the moistness in her eyes and asked, tentatively, "Hi, is this Darcy Whiteman?"

There was a slight pause on the other end, and then the woman answered, "Yes, it is. Who's this?"

"My name is Zaina Whiteman. I'm your daughter."

The pause that followed was three times as long as the one that came before it. The next time the woman named Darcy spoke, her voice was thick and strained, as if she was suppressing a sob. "You're... you're one of the quints?" she asked.

"Yes... Mom. And I've got the others with me. Well, most of them, anyway. Cristiano and Sage."

"May I talk to them?" Now Darcy definitely sounded like she was crying. There was no mistaking that slight whimper at the back of her throat or the faint sniffles that could be heard on the other end of the line.

Zaina nodded, though she knew Darcy couldn't see her. Then she took the phone and pattered back into the office, where Cristiano and Sage were still poring over the computer screen.

The phone was passed around during the next few minutes, and long pent-up tears, conversations, and laughter were exchanged before Zaina was nudged by Cristiano into dropping the bomb. He handed her the phone, then stood by to watch and wait.

Nervously, Zaina spoke into the phone. "Uh, Mom?" She tried to swallow past her nerves before continuing. "Can you and Dad... uh... do us a favor?"

"Are you kidding?" Darcy actually chuckled. "After all these years, your father and I owe you kids a *million* favors. What is it, sweetheart?"

Zaina didn't know what to say. Where would she even start? Somehow, she couldn't bring herself to tell Darcy the truth about Alaric. After all, reuniting with the children she gave up almost thirty years ago is plenty to take in by itself.

On the other hand, Darcy might have a heart attack or something if she knew what one of her sons was up to.

So, Zaina decided to skate around the issue.

"Would you and Dad want to come down to Central Park tomorrow afternoon? I read that you're living in Syracuse... NYC isn't that far from there, is it? And I think Alaric and Astraea will be there too... anyway, I just think it'd be nice if we could all meet there, have a real in-person reunion."

Darcy Whiteman didn't hesitate longer than two seconds to say, "Oh, we'd love to!"

In the background, Juniper, the quintuplets' jovial, kind-voiced father added, "We'll be there!"

And so, the plan was formed.

Cristiano, Sage, and Zaina were going to New York City. They were going to meet their parents, stop Alaric, save Astraea, and hopefully, save the world.

Chapter Six
New York City

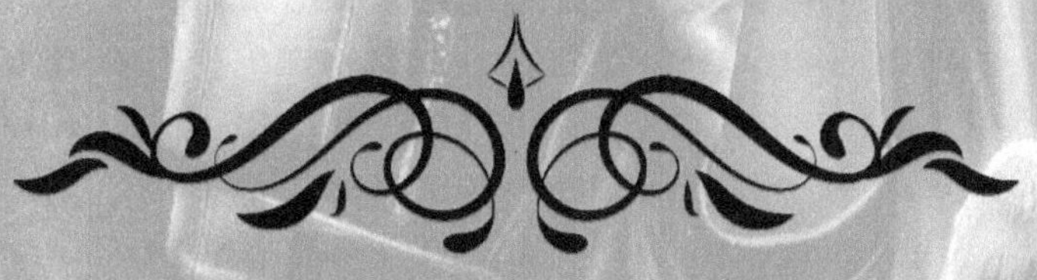

The airplane was cold and crowded with people traveling for the holidays, but Zaina was flushed with excitement. She sat next to her husband, with Bord and Sage's daughter sitting together behind them. Cristiano, Sage, and Ria were elsewhere on the plane, all strapped and ready for the journey to New York City.

Within a few minutes, the plane lifted into the air. Zaina's heart dropped into her stomach from the sudden rise. This was her first time being on an actual plane. She'd usually just fly to wherever she needed to go.

But that wasn't the only reason. Fear churned in her gut like a looming storm. What would happen when they landed?

Would their suspicions be correct—would they find Astraea and Alaric there? And would they be able to convince them to change their ways? Part of her was tempted to turn back, to go back to her comfortable, peaceful life in the woods and let the rest of the world deal with Alaric's evilness.

But she couldn't do that. She owed it to her siblings to step up to the plate, to make up for her childhood mistake.

Sage leaned his head back against the airplane seat and tried to calm his nervous jitters as the drink cart rolled by. He always had them—it was his body's constant need for a physical movement that spurred them on. Normally, he could go outside for a run or head to the field to coach his football team. But now, he was forced to sit still and think.

Alaric doesn't stand a chance. We'll bring him to our side in no time.

Forever an optimist, Sage felt certain that this trip would end with a resounding success. He believed in the power of hope, of family, and most importantly, of the power each of his siblings possessed.

We've got this in the bag.

He smiled to himself and imagined the twenty-year-old version of himself, sprinting across a green field to catch a football hurtling through the air.

Touchdown, he thought to himself. *Just like this will be.*

Cristiano's fingers flew across the keyboard, typing so fast that the laptop balanced on his knees quivered.

I won't be coming into the office tomorrow. He wrote to his supervisor, *on an investigation in NYC. May be something, may be nothing. Just want to monitor things until I know for sure. I'll keep you posted.*

He sent the email, then waved away the flight attendant offering him a glass of champagne. Now was not the time.

Just when the flight attendant left, Cristiano's laptop beeped with a new notification. An email came in—straight from his supervisor's desk.

What's up, Cristiano? What do you think is going on? Terrorists?

Worse, Cristiano typed back, *my brother.*

With a sigh, he closed his laptop and leaned back in his chair, hoping his intuition would be wrong for once.

A couple hours later, the plane landed in the bustling heart of New York City. Zaina, Cristiano, and Sage landed at the airport, accompanied by their families, and headed straight for the hotel they booked. There, they got settled with a shower, a change of clothes, and a nice hot meal.

First, Zaina called Juniper and Darcy to let them know the three of them had arrived safely. Then she called her brothers' rooms and declared an official family meeting. Now that half of their journey was over, a plan was in order.

Later that evening, Cristiano, Sage, and Zaina took the elevator to the ground floor and met each other in the lobby's corner, where a set of plush armchairs flanked a fireplace and several tall, picture windows that overlooked the sprawling city ahead of them.

"Hey, guys," Sage, who arrived last, strode towards the two siblings sitting in silence by the fire, a big smile on his face as always. "Man, isn't this great? We're in NYC! Always wanted to come here." He took the empty seat beside Cristiano, then peered at each of their faces, noticing their matching glum expressions. "What's up?"

"It's seven o'clock," Zaina said. "We have less than twenty-four hours before we'll be seeing Alaric and Astraea again. We need to formulate a plan."

Sage frowned. "I thought we already had a plan. Didn't we say having Alaric meet with our birth parents was going to solve everything?"

Zaina bit her lip. "I'm not so sure about that anymore. It may fix part of the problem, but not all of it."

Worry took over Sage's normally jovial face. He watched his little sister, with a cloud of fear in his eyes.

She continued, "I've been thinking about everything that happened twenty years ago. Alaric always had a little bit of bad in him. Still, things never really escalated until he met that old man who told him about the purple diamond. Remember?"

With a faraway look in his eyes, Cristiano nodded. "The diamond changed everything. We should have never left it behind for him—we should have destroyed it."

"But how could we have known?" Zaina asked. "We were just kids. We thought it was an awesome thing, the way it enhanced all our powers like it did. But you guys, I've realized something. Suppose the diamond is powerful enough to increase our abilities and free Alaric from his prison inside the cave.

What else is it capable of? It could have some kind of hold on Alaric, and we wouldn't even know. It might not be the real him anymore—he might be possessed by the diamond."

Silence. It was so thick for a while that all they could hear was the low crackling of the fire. Some people who had walked past just as Zaina was giving her speech cast wary, yet halfway amused, looks at the siblings, probably assuming they were part of some book club discussing a fantasy novel. They had no idea what lurked beneath their perception of reality.

"Okay, let's think about this," Sage said. "Maybe Darcy and Juniper's love will be enough to break the diamond's grip on Alaric. After all, they're our parents, the family he's always wanted. But maybe it won't. We need to have a backup plan in case it doesn't."

Cristiano nodded. "We need to destroy the diamond. Once and for all."

"How? How would we even know where he keeps the thing? It could be anywhere!"

"No." Somehow, Zaina sensed the answer to this was a lot simpler than that. "He'll have it with him. If the thing is as powerful as we think it is, Alaric won't be able to let it out of his sight. When we were ten, I remember he used to hang the thing around his neck, like a necklace."

"Great." Sage threw his hands up. "He'll burn us to the ground if we even think about getting that close to him!"

"Maybe not," Cristiano said, a strange glint in his eyes. "I have an idea."

"What is it?" Sage screeched. "Let it out, boy!"

Cristiano said, "We'll be actors. Alaric didn't come to kill us, remember? He came because he wanted us to join him. It's that craving for family deep down inside him, like you said, Zaina. So maybe, if we pretend to have a change of heart, if we go to him and act like we want to join his side like Astraea, we'll have a chance to get close to him. Then we could grab the diamond, destroy it, and be done with all this craziness."

Both Sage and Zaina gazed at their brother with awe.

"Wow, Cristiano," Zaina said, smiling. "That's a brilliant idea."

"One question," Sage said, holding up a finger. "How exactly do we destroy the diamond? I mean, it's obviously not a normal diamond."

Cristiano nodded in agreement. "It'll definitely take power."

Zaina gasped and held her hand over her mouth. "Astraea!" she exclaimed.

"Yes." Cristiano dipped his head forward in a nod, and the firelight reflected off his hair with bright orange color. "Astraea's the only one with the power to destroy the diamond."

Chapter Seven
The Plan

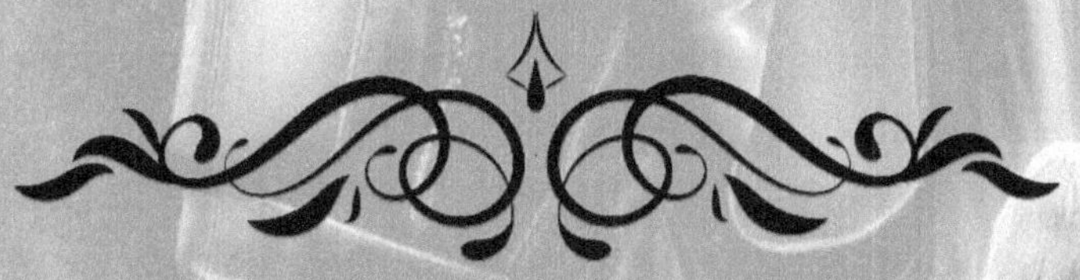

Alaric stood by the tall floor-to-ceiling window in his hotel room, fingers pressed to the cool glass, and watched the snow fall over Central Park. He was amazed at all the people gathered there, thousands of them milling about on the snow-covered green, skating like they don't have a care in the world. It would be the perfect place to start his plan of influence.

After this, he'd move on to every state in the country, every capital city, where the crowds were many, and the people were open-minded. Chicago, Atlanta, Los Angeles, Miami. He had already bought the plane tickets—it was only a matter of time before the whole country was in the palm of his hand. And then... the whole *world.*

He turned around and smiled at the woman seated on the couch behind him. Astraea. His guarantee for success.

"How you feeling, sis?" he asked.

"Wonderful, Alaric." Her voice, dense and emotionless, confirmed to Alaric that the trance was still working. She was still his to use as he wished—all thanks to his number one prized possession.

Grinning to himself, he rotated again, facing the window once more, and his hand went up to touch the purple gemstone hanging around his neck. The pendant was attached to a long chain that could be safely hidden beneath his shirt. It clung to his chest, where it had laid for so many years now.

It was practically an extension of his own body. He stroked it fondly, watching the crowds gather under the late morning sun. Just a few more hours.... just a few more hours...

The siblings woke up early after a night of restless, nightmare-filled sleep. Once they got dressed in the December darkness, they went downstairs for coffee and breakfast.

But a surprise was waiting for them in the lobby.

The moment the three of them stepped off the elevator and onto the clean tiled floor, they were greeted by an elderly couple wearing identical nervous smiles. The woman was plump and petite, her silvery hair cut into a wavy bob that framed her face with thick, pretty curls. The man was jovial with a white beard like Santa Claus and had his arm wrapped around the woman's shoulders.

Zaina couldn't believe her eyes. She knew, deep inside, that these weren't ordinary people. They were her parents. Her biological mother and father.

Her nerves were instantly whisked away by wonder and joy. "Darcy and Juniper?" she asked tentatively.

"Yes, sweetheart." A tear rolled down the gray-haired woman's cheek. "It's us."

Though the siblings had already spoken to their parents over the phone, they never could have prepared themselves for the overwhelming emotions that took over the moment they actually met them in person.

Secretly, they'd all dreamt of this moment from the time they were little kids and learned they'd been separated from their birth parents. And now... that dream was finally coming true.

The tears were even stronger than they had been over the phone. Even Cristiano, who never showed any emotion, let alone shed a tear, was crying like a baby. The five gathered at a circular table in the hotel's dining area. They shared thirty years' worth of stories over coffee, donuts, and blueberry muffins.

Darcy and Juniper were extremely apologetic at the mistake they'd made in their youth. They spoke with blatant remorse in their eyes as they recalled their feelings thirty years ago when the children first showed signs of their abilities.

At the time, giving them up had seemed like the only option—they'd been terrified at the thought of someone finding out and coming to kidnap or kill them.

They described these things like a sheepish child confessing a wrong done behind her mother's back. But, despite the regrets their parents had, there was no animosity in any of the siblings' hearts.

"We don't blame you at all," Sage said, clapping his father on the back. "I mean, it hurts, of course, knowing that we missed out on so many years with you. But we all had good lives, and we understand that it must have been scary at the time, you two being so young, giving birth to five kids with supernatural powers."

"Yeah," Zaina agreed. "I mean, I was terrified enough when Bord was born, and he's only one kid! And not even a supernatural one!"

"Oh!" Darcy beamed and clapped her hands together, her blue eyes shining. "I have grandchildren?"

"Two!" Sage declared with a grin. "And they're both upstairs with our wives. Well, *my* wife, Ria, and Zaina's husband, Theo. Poor Cristiano here is still single."

"Oh, I can't wait to meet them. But... what about Astraea? And Alaric? Do they have any children?"

At the mention of the duo they were up against, Zaina, Cristiano, and Sage all faltered, stiffening in their chairs.

"Um, no," Zaina said. "As far as I know, they're both still single. Astraea is a, um, magician in Las Vegas. Alaric is..."

Helplessly, she looked at her brothers, silently begging them to help her. She didn't know what the heck she was supposed to say.

Sage, catching her signal, spoke up at that moment. Still, he was as bold and straightforward as always, the thought of sugarcoating things or beating around the bush never even crossing his mind.

"Oh, Alaric's evil," he said. "I don't think he has a job unless scheming to take over the entire world counts."

Darcy and Juniper both looked horrified. The most uncomfortable silence in the entire world descended over their breakfast table.

Oh well, Zaina thought, *at least the truth's out now. Might as well run with it.*

She took it upon herself to fill their parents in on the situation, starting the long story right at the very beginning, when the quints were ten, newly discovering their powers, and battling their devious brother, Alaric.

This was not only the first time Juniper and Darcy were hearing the truth about their son. It was also the first time they witnessed their children's powers in over two decades.

They were both stunned and delighted to watch Zaina levitate over the table. Cristiano made himself invisible in his chair, and Sage tapped into his speed to dart from one end of the lobby to the other in only a half-second's time.

But then the elderly couple had no choice but to acknowledge the impossible—their son was evil.

"I... I can't believe this." Darcy sat back in her chair with a dazed look on her face.

Zaina eyed her anxiously. "You're not... you don't regret meeting us, do you?"

Darcy's eyes widened. "Oh no! Not at all, honey." She reached across the table to stroke Zaina's smooth hand with her wrinkled one. "There's no room for regret—only joy. I'm just... shocked. I mean, I never imagined that any of my children would turn out bad. It's horrible, what's become of Alaric. Is that why you all came here? To try to stop him?"

The siblings nodded gravely.

"And that's why we got in touch with you guys," Sage interjected. "Alaric has always been desperate to find you. We thought that if we brought you two to him, he'd have a change of heart."

Juniper's face clouded over. Just like his son, Sage, he had a tendency to wear a perpetual, beaming expression. So, it was extra jarring when he frowned. The seriousness of the circumstance weighed over all of them, the intensity clear in each of their gazes as they stared at each other.

Finally, Darcy said, "We will help in any way we can. It's the least we can do after so many years of not being in your lives. I'm not sure if we'll be any good against magic and diamonds and all that, but we'll give it our best shot. Right, Juniper?"

He gave a sharp nod in response. "Of course."

With pale smiles, the siblings sipped their cold, neglected coffee. They nibbled on their stale muffins, reveling in the first glimpses of hope they'd experienced yet.

They still had a chance. Even though it seemed impossible, nothing was over until it was over. And now, they had two more people on their side.

They were ready to face Alaric.

Chapter Eight
Powers Unleashed

The occasion was the annual Holiday in the Park event, a festival of sorts, full of music, food, and fellowship.

A big stage had been set up for bands and jazz musicians to perform classic Christmas songs all night long. Right now, at five after six, a blond woman and a man in an ugly Christmas sweater were singing a duet to the cheers of the thousands watching them from the plastic chairs upfront.

Many others milled about the park, visiting Santa and Mrs. Claus with their children, sipping hot chocolate and eating funnel cakes sold by the happy-faced vendors, and chattering with their friends and family beneath the snowflakes drifting down.

Zaina, Cristiano, and Sage hovered at the entrance, their parents, spouses, and children by their sides.

"Mommy, I want to go see Santa!" Ava cried, tugging on Ria's arm.

With the same enthusiasm, Bord appealed to Zaina, begging to join Ava.

"You guys do what you have to do," Ria said, looking first at her husband, then at the others. "I'll take the kids to see Santa."

Sage gave her a quick but loving kiss on the lips, holding her hand close to him before letting it go. "Thanks, sweetheart. I'd prefer they not be in the vicinity, just in case... something goes wrong."

Ria nodded with understanding, then, with one hand holding Ava's and the other holding Bord's, she marched off through the snow, heading for the North Pole display that had been set up right between the mass of chairs and one of the food trucks.

"I'll go too," Theo said, touching Zaina's arm. "Just to make sure Bord doesn't get into any trouble."

Smiling at the thought of their rambunctious son, Zaina nodded gratefully.

She said, "Thanks, Theo," and then watched him stride away, following Ria's footprints.

The five of them were left alone. After a moment, they walked further into the park, then veered off to the side, away from the most crowded path. Here, hidden from the majority of the gatherers, they hashed out their plan.

"Alright," Zaina said. "I think we should approach Alaric first before we let him meet Mom and Dad. But we need to be extra careful around Astraea—now that we're close by, she'll be able to read our minds and know if we're truthful or not. Make sure you're paying attention to what you're thinking about. Try as hard as you can to only think about joining Alaric. Otherwise, that lie will fall apart before it even gets started."

Cristiano and Sage nodded.

Then Sage asked, "Who's going to be in charge of getting the diamond?"

"Me," Zaina said. "I'll use my telekinesis to get it off his neck—but then I'll have to convince Astraea to destroy it."

"Just tell him Alaric wants her to do it," Sage suggested. "Say it's because he wants to get rid of the evidence."

Zaina winced. "You really think that'll work?"

Sage shrugged. "It's worth a shot."

"What do we do when Alaric realizes the thing's not around his neck anymore? It definitely won't take him long before he notices."

Zaina nodded at Cristiano's question. "Well, my hope is that, once it's off of him, the enchantment will be broken, and he won't be as... well, evil. But if all else fails, we can use brute force to stave him off until Astraea has time to destroy the thing. You're super strong and fast, Sage. You can take him, right?"

"Of course! Remember? We battled it out when we were kids, and I totally won." With full confidence, Sage smiled and flexed his muscles. "That bony little weasel is no match for me!"

Zaina smiled at his endearing cockiness. "Okay, but just remember... he *does* have powers. Just be fast—take him by surprise. Then, once the diamond is destroyed, Mom and Dad can come in and do their thing. Sound good?"

"In theory, yes," Cristiano said.

With a sigh, Zaina said, "Well, theory's the best option we've got right now. It's either that or stand by while Alaric takes over the whole world. We just have to work with what we've got."

Nods passed among their group, and then Darcy asked, "So, when is this all starting?"

"Any minute now." Zaina glanced towards the stage. "After these people finish performing, another band is scheduled to come on in fifteen minutes. After that, there'll be an intermission, and we're pretty sure that's when Alaric is planning to hop on stage and hypnotize everyone.

Right now, we need to scope out the place and see if we can find them before that happens."

"How about we split up?" Sage suggested. "Dad, Mom, and I can go together, and you and Cristiano can go together."

"Alright."

Once they were all in agreement, they abandoned their little hiding spot and went their separate ways.

They walked around the park for several minutes, keeping their eyes peeled for any sign of Alaric or Astraea, but they never spotted either of them.

It wasn't until Zaina spotted a woman with long brown hair standing by the giant Christmas tree in the center of the park, reaching up to touch one of the huge twinkling ornaments, that hope stirred in her chest. Though she couldn't be sure, the woman's silhouette looked very familiar. Could it be Astraea?

"I think I found them," Zaina hissed at Cristiano, grabbing his arm and pointing in the direction of the Christmas tree.

Her finger aimed at the brown-haired girl and the guy standing beside her. When Cristiano looked up, the guy turned, and Cristiano and Zaina got a full front view of his face.

It was Alaric.

Though her nerves were frayed and her heartbeat pounded at a million miles an hour, Zaina smiled.

She turned to Cristiano and said, "Alright, we need to distract Alaric. Do you think you can use your invisibility to do something?"

"I'm on it," Cristiano said, and then he immediately disappeared.

Zaina gasped. Cristiano's power would never get any less jarring.

Through wide, unblinking eyes, she watched the prints appear in the snow by invisible feet. They darted toward the Christmas tree ahead, just inches from where Alaric stood, before disappearing.

She frowned. Where did Cristiano go? Why did the prints disappear?

She was on the verge of getting nervous... but then it happened.

There was a rustle at the top of the tree, where the giant, lighted star was placed.

Zaina's jaw dropped as the star was pushed off by an invisible force and dashed straight towards the top of Alaric's head.

Nice one, Cristiano! She thought, just before the heavy metal star crashed down on Alaric, knocking him to the ground with a thud that could be heard even from where she was standing.

Zaina watched Astraea turn, in shock, to face Alaric—and then Zaina started forward with a swift run. She dashed as fast as she could towards Astraea's side, peeking out of the corner of her eye at Alaric, who still lied on the floor, groaning.

Just before she reached Astraea, Zaina flung out her hand and pictured the purple diamond in her mind, imagining it breaking away from the chain around Alaric's neck and soaring into her palm. She was grateful her telekinesis powers were fast. There was almost no delay before the glistening purple crystal came flying at her like a rogue baseball.

With a sharp breath, she leaped into the air and caught it, then shoved it safely down in her coat pocket.

Oh, thank goodness.

But she couldn't rejoice yet. She still had Astraea to worry about.

She reached her sister, breathless, and yanked hard on her arm, pulling her around to the other side of the tree before Astraea even had time to realize what happened.

Somewhere above her, Cristiano stood, unseen, at the top of the Christmas tree, watching the events unfold on the ground below him and getting ready to send more ornaments toppling down on Alaric's head, should he get up at the wrong time.

But Cristiano was out of Zaina's head. Astraea turned around to face her with a fast, whipping motion, and her eyes blazed with fire.

"Zaina. Traitor of Alaric," she said and then raised her hand.

But Zaina composed her thoughts and cried out, "Wait!" right before Astraea used her magic against her. Then, desperately, she cried out, "I'm on your side, Astraea.

You and Alaric. I came because I want to join you guys."

Astraea blinked and stepped back as if she'd been slapped across the face. Some clarity beamed through the fog in her eyes.

"Seriously?" When Zaina nodded, a smirk slid across Astraea's face. "I knew it," she said. "I knew you'd eventually turn back to your ten-year-old ways."

Zaina fought the urge to think negative thoughts in response and slapped a bright smile on her face instead. "Yeah! I made a mistake when I left Alaric all those years ago."

Astraea grinned. "Well, let's go tell him!"

She started forward, but Zaina grabbed her arm to stop her. "Wait," she said, flashing a panicked glance at Alaric. He was still on the ground, moaning in pain and snapping at the few people passing by who asked if he needed an ambulance.

Looking back at Astraea, she said, "I already told Alaric. He's... he's super excited. And he already gave me my first mission."

"Ooh, what is it?"

Taking a deep breath, Zaina reached into her pocket and pulled out the purple diamond. Terror flitted through her at the thought of giving it over to Astraea, but she had to trust her plan. This was the only way they'd be able to destroy the stone.

She handed it to Astraea and said, "Alaric wants you to destroy this. See, he wants to eliminate any evidence that might link him back to... back to what he's about to do. Of course, he'd do it himself, but you know, your magic is way greater than his."

At first, Astraea frowned. The skepticism was as blatant on her face as the fear was in Zaina's chest. But then Astraea's expression smoothed over. She nodded in agreement.

"Alright," she said with a shrug. "Well, if that's what Alaric wants, then, of course, I'll do it."

"Yeah." Zaina smiled. "And, uh, he said he wants you to do it right now. Sooner the better, and all that. Better do it before he gets up."

"Oh, okay. Sure!" Taking the bait perfectly, Astraea held the purple diamond in her open palm. Narrowing her eyes at the shiny gem, she hovered her free hand above it. Zaina was practically hypnotized as she watched the magic flow out of Astraea's fingertips.

They slithered out like smoky snakes and fog ribbons. The magic surrounded the stone in Astraea's palm for one second— then cleared completely, leaving only emptiness behind. Astraea's palm was bare—she'd totally erased the purple diamond from the atmosphere.

Zaina smiled at her sister, relief and joy crashing through her.

But things got even better when Zaina saw the haziness leave Astraea's gaze as suddenly as if she'd been doused with water. Astraea came back to Earth with rapid blinks, her eyebrows furrowing in confusion as she looked around.

Her eyes finally found Zaina. "Zaina?" she asked. "What's going on?"

Zaina frowned. "What do you mean?"
"Is this Central Park? What the heck am I doing here?"

Zaina's mind swam with the reality of the situation. The loud music, the buzz of activity around her, the groans of Alaric in the background—it was all so overwhelming. But one sliver of truth, one shocking discovery, slipped through the chaos and into her awareness.

Astraea had never been on Alaric's side! Not willingly, anyway. It was just his power and the purple diamond, putting her in a trance. Now that the diamond was destroyed, Astraea's trance was broken. Did that mean Alaric's evilness would dissipate too?

Without even bothering to fill Astraea in on the situation, she whizzed around to face Alaric, just as he was getting up from the ground. A glass ball that Cristiano kicked towards him came tumbling down the Christmas tree, but this time, Alaric saw it and stepped out of the way just in time.

As the glass shattered on the snow, turning its pure-white surface glittery with silver, Alaric looked up, flung out his hand, and commanded, "Show yourself, brother!"

The blast of lightning that shot out of his palm both exposed Cristiano and sent him hurling out of his perch atop the tree. Zaina cried out as her brother hit the ground with a heavy thud. The tree was at least fifty feet tall—would Cristiano be okay?

There was no time to find out. As soon as she screamed, Alaric whirled towards the sound and caught sight of her for the first time that night. He snarled like a hungry beast cornering its prey.

"Hello, Zaina," he said. "Trying to stop me, are you? Well, good luck with that. Astraea's under my power now. Astraea, pulverize both of them."

"Excuse me?" In shock, Astraea looked at Alaric like he was nuts, eyes bulging out of her face. "Listen here, kid. I'm not under your power! And I will *not* pulverize my brother and sister!"

"Fine, I'll do it myself." Smirking, Alaric outstretched his hand again, but this time, he stopped himself before going further. "Wait. You're not... under my power anymore? How is that possible?"

Accusatory eyes flitted to Zaina's face, narrowing with intensity. "None of you dorks have the power to do something like that. What's the meaning of this?"

Then, as he noticed the void beneath his shirt that had been taken up by the diamond for so many years, Alaric clapped a hand to his chest. Horror turned his face three different shades of ghostly pale white.

Finally, like a mother who had lost her child, he stammered in panic, "My—my—m-my diamond... where is it, what have you done with it?"

Zaina actually felt sorry for him. She hated seeing her brother upset, even if he deserved it.

But that didn't last long when she saw Cristiano writhing in pain on the floor. In the distance, she spotted Sage with their parents. They'd all caught sight of each other, and the three of them were rushing forward now. Zaina's heart soared for all of them. Her poor family... Alaric had tried to destroy them. He didn't deserve her pity.

"The jig is up, brother!" she said. "Your precious diamond is destroyed! Astraea used her magic to get rid of it. Now you're only half as powerful as you were before."

A growl emitted from Alaric's lips. "Oh, you shouldn't have done that," he whispered. "Only half as powerful, huh? That's still plenty enough to demolish you!"

With that, he flung both his arms up into the air, and immediately, the elements obeyed his movements. The peacefully drifting snow turned savage, accelerating into a biting, icy blizzard that assaulted everyone in the park.

Alaric waved his arms even more, and the winds obeyed, blowing so fast and harshly that the Christmas tree wobbled, nearly toppling over on several passersby. People started screaming and running, hurrying to the entrance as they called things out like, "It's a tornado!" "It's a blizzard!"

All the while, Alaric stood in the middle of the blizzard, totally unharmed, a conductor orchestrating the whole thing.

Zaina feared for her son and husband. Alaric had turned the fluffy snow into a hard, sharp, hail-like substance. It bit through her clothes and cut her skin, making painful stings all over her body.

"Alaric, stop it!" she shouted, praying her family would vacate in time before they got seriously injured.

Beside her, Astraea was casting out bolts of magic, but they fizzled out the moment they left her hands. The snow extinguished them as if they were mere candle flames.

Alaric laughed, his cackles echoing around the empty park.

But then, all of a sudden, two people materialized out of the blizzard, Darcy and Juniper Whiteman.

At the same time, they both clamped a hand on Alaric's shoulder.

And Juniper said, in a low but not unkind voice, "That's enough of that, son."

Chapter Nine
The Diamond Destroyed

The blizzard stopped. The winds calmed. The snowflakes slowed.

Peace loomed over Central Park once more, arms hovering over the heads of the bystanders as if expecting more turmoil to appear.

Slowly, his eyes widened, his skin pale. Finally, Alaric turned around and faced his parents for the first time.

"Mom?" he whispered. "Dad?"

With tears streaming down her face, Darcy nodded. "Yes, Alaric. It's us."

Juniper said, "We've been waiting to meet you for a long time, son."

Zaina's shoulders sagged with relief as she watched Darcy and Juniper lead Alaric away from the scene, towards the chairs flanking the stage where they sat down for a long and overdue heart-to-heart. She hoped the conversation would go well.

But then her thoughts were consumed with the rest of her family.

She immediately started towards Cristiano, who had yet to get off the ground. She and Astraea both crouched down on the bare patches of snow where the glass hadn't touched and hovered over him.

"Oh, Cristiano," Zaina said, touching his cheek. "Please be okay."

Almost immediately after the words escaped her, Cristiano jolted up as if she'd recited a resurrection spell.

"I'm fine, you guys," he said, cracking a smile. "I was just pretending to be dead."

Zaina was so overwhelmed with relief that she tossed her arms around his neck and nearly crushed him with the force from her hug. Then she and Astraea each grabbed one of his arms and hauled him to his feet, where Sage waited to clap him on the shoulder.

"Nice going with the Christmas tree ornaments, dude. That was totally epic!" he said.

A glimmer of pride shined through Cristiano's grin. "Thanks."

"You guys, I'm so sorry for turning against you; I had no idea what I was doing," Astraea said, grabbing everyone's attention with one short sentence.

Turning toward her, the three siblings watched as Astraea's eyes filled with tears. Her bottom lip quivered as she said, "I just can't believe Alaric used me like that! I can't believe I *let* him."

"It's not your fault, Astraea," Zaina said, reaching out to stroke her sister's shoulder. "He had you under a trance—you couldn't have stopped it."

Astraea nodded and gave a little sniffle. "Thanks, guys. Especially you, Zaina. Thank you for snapping me out of it."

"No problem. You did the same thing for me, remember? Twenty years ago, when *I* was the idiot who got persuaded by Alaric? Astraea, you were the one who snapped me out of *my* trance and brought me back to my senses. I figured it was time to return the favor."

The tense energy dissipated from the cold air as the four of them shared a light laugh. The moment passed between them like the warmth of a spring breeze. Then, naturally, they all shifted their bodies, turning toward the seating arena. The multitude of chairs looked eerie in the empty space. Now that Central Park had become a ghost town in under two seconds, the air itself held a creepy note.

But three chairs were taken up. Zaina, Cristiano, Sage, and Astraea stared at the people on them, wondering how the talk between Alaric and their parents was going. However, they didn't *look* upset. In fact, Darcy actually had a small smile on her face as she nodded at whatever Alaric was saying.

"Guys, I think...." Zaina hesitated, whispering as if daring to voice her thoughts might jinx the possibility of salvation. "I think our plan worked. Alaric has always just been a vulnerable little boy in need of his parents' love. Now that he has it..."

Sage finished her thought with a question. "You really think it's over? You think he'll be on the straight and narrow now?"

Just then, the three people on the chairs rose to their feet, turned, and started toward the siblings with quick, purposeful strides. Alaric walked between Darcy and Juniper, holding his mother's hand while his father kept one strong, steady hand on his shoulder. Alaric had never looked so young, so childlike. He'd also never looked so happy.

"Yeah, I really think so," Zaina answered with a grin.

When the mother, father, and son trio came to a halt in front of the siblings, Alaric immediately lifted his eyes to each of them. His gaze was full of emotions—guilt, remorse, and fear being the most prominent.

As he stared at his brothers and sisters, he thought of what he wanted to say. He conjured up a million words to describe how sorry he was, how much he regretted the past thirty years, how he didn't deserve a do-over but wanted one more than anything, how grateful he was that his siblings cared enough about him even though he'd never returned the gesture.

But when he opened his mouth, only three of those million words actually came out.

"I'm so sorry, guys," he said.

But that was enough. And without hesitating one more second, the siblings smiled and reached for Alaric, pulling him into a group hug so tight that it warmed them all up from the inside out, like they had their own personal fireplace nestled between them to stave off the winter air.

"This is officially the best Christmas ever," Astraea cheered.

"On the contrary, this is the *worst* Christmas ever," a strange voice suddenly said.

They hadn't even heard the stranger approach. Though the ground was covered in snow that crunched when they stepped on it, the owner of the gruff, male voice seemed to appear out of nowhere, materializing from thin air without ever creating any footsteps.

Darcy and Juniper gasped. One by one, the siblings let go of each other and turned around slowly, their stomachs churning with dread.

"No, it can't be," Alaric whispered.

The old man stood before them. Alaric hadn't seen him in years, for which he was grateful. The evil man, perpetually immortal and frozen at age seventy, had started everything bad in Alaric's life, beginning with the moment he enticed him to steal the purple diamond.

As always, the old man was flanked by his huge wolf servant, and he looked at everything through narrow, smirking eyes.

"Hello, Alaric," he said. "Long time no see."

With a wave of his hand, Alaric urged his parents and siblings to stay back. Striding forward on his own, he stepped in front of them all, facing the old man by himself.

"What are you doing here?" he demanded with rage.

The old man leisurely caressed the wolf by his side while his intense stare scrutinized Alaric. "You've changed," said the old man. "I can sense it."

"Yes," Alaric confirmed. "But why are you here? You haven't approached me since I was ten. I thought you were dead."

"I sensed a large portion of my powers draining out," the old man confessed. All around him, snow fell, drifting onto his head and skin, but he ignored it.

Seemingly unperturbed by the cold or anything, he stood tall and calm in a short-sleeve shirt despite the temperature. "You've destroyed my purple diamond, haven't you?"

"*Your* purple diamond?" Astraea asked, speaking up in shock as she moved forward to stand beside Alaric.

"Of course, it's mine." The old man gave Astraea a disdainful look. "The purple diamond contains all of my essence, all of my energy. Unfortunately, I was cursed centuries ago, so I could not keep the diamond in possession myself. Therefore, I instructed you, young Alaric, to steal it and hold it for me, ensuring it would always be in safekeeping," he finished with an evil smile, turning his head towards Alaric.

Zaina sucked in a breath. She had no idea destroying the diamond would have such repercussions. Who was this old man, anyway? And how did he get cursed? How could a tiny gem hold all of his powers?

"Now I can see that you were never the right person to trust the diamond with," the old man continued, rage forming in his eyes. "After all, you destroyed the one thing equivalent to my lifeblood. You erased eighty percent of my powers."

Alaric shifted his weight, fidgeting nervously with the hem of his shirt. His eyes darted back and forth between the old man and the wolf at his side.

In the old days, Alaric had been best friends with that wolf. He'd communicated with a lot of animals during the course of his young life, but none of them had understood him the same way that wolf had. During the brief time they were together, they used to joke that they were kindred spirits. But now... the wolf probably had forgotten that.

Instead, he would most likely be on the old man's side and tear Alaric to pieces the moment he was commanded to.

"You're not the only one," Alaric said. "A significant chunk of my powers was destroyed as well. But now I've changed my ways. Maybe you should do the same."

"Actually, I have no intentions of doing that." A sly smile spread across the old man's tan, wrinkly face. "My plan is to take back what you stole from me. After all, my magic sustains me. Without it, I'll die."

"You *should* die!" Alaric snapped. "You're, like, a million years old! Stop fighting fate already—it's not natural."

The old man continued to smile. It was unnerving, the way he didn't show any anger. Only his eyes told the truth; there were shadows in them that couldn't be masked.

"Don't worry," he said, addressing all the quints now, letting his dark eyes skate over each of their faces. "It won't hurt. In fact, it will be quite fast and painless."

Fast and painless? Zaina's breath hitched in her throat. What was about to happen to her, to all of them?

Suddenly, the man lifted one hand towards the five siblings. In response to this, Astraea moved like lightning, gathering up the power within her. But she wasn't fast enough. Despite his age, frail appearance, and claim of losing huge amounts of his power, the old man was a formidable force.

He used his magic to freeze the quintuplets, paralyzing them with nothing more than a flutter of his fingers, just like Alaric had.

"There, that should keep you still while I drain your powers."

What? No!

He can't do that. He's not that powerful.

Oh man, what'll I do without my speed and strength?

We have to stop him! But my magic won't work —

If only we still had that diamond...

All at once, a thousand thoughts danced through each of the siblings' minds. But they couldn't do anything about the enchantment holding them in place. Their limbs felt like stone sculptures, solid, stiff, and incapable of movement. No matter how hard they tried to break free from the spell, they were completely powerless.

The old man chuckled. "So cute, how you've all banded together now. I had no idea you were such a softie, Alaric. Who would've guessed that all it would take for you to change your ways was a hug from your mommy and daddy? How sweet. Unfortunately, I've never liked sweet things."

Just then, the old man pointed a finger at Alaric's chest, and he was immediately overcome with a horrible numbing sensation that crept and crawled all over his body. It wasn't pain, not exactly, but that didn't make it any less uncomfortable.

The worst thing was, he couldn't do anything about it; still paralyzed, he could do nothing but let the weird and awful feeling course through his body, wave after wave, each one more terrible than the last.

That's when it happened. A thin ribbon of light, glowing bright blue, pierced through Alaric's chest from deep inside his soul. The old man flexed his fingers, coaxing the ribbon further until it left Alaric's body entirely.

The string of light, which Alaric recognized as the source of his supernatural powers, flew across the snowy park and landed on the old man's palm. There, it sunk into his skin, and all of Alaric's powers were absorbed inside the one who had stolen it.

Alaric dropped to the ground, breathless. He was so shocked by what had just happened that he barely even realized the spell paralyzing him had worn off. As if he had a hole inside him, a horrible, hollow feeling clawed at his chest. He grasped at his heart, though he knew it was too late. There was no way of restoring his power. It belonged to the old man now.

"Thank you, Alaric," the old man said cheerily as if Alaric had willingly given up his powers.

His eyes then darted over to the others. He looked at each of the siblings before letting his gaze linger on Astraea—his next target.

"Yes. You're the one who has both magic and mind-reading abilities. Your powers will make the perfect addition."

Astraea only had time to let out a mental shriek in her head before she succumbed to the same fate that just consumed her brother, her soul ripping out of her chest.

Suddenly, all she knew were the tingly chills ravaging her body, reaching inside her for the powers that made her who she was. If she hadn't been paralyzed, she would've been crying.

What would she do without her magic? How could she continue her career as a magician? Would she end up homeless?

Pretty soon, even her fearful thoughts were overpowered by the mind-blowing scene of the glowing thread pushing through her chest and leaving her body. It was the strangest thing to see. She'd never imagined that her magic could actually have a physical form like that—to her mind, it had always been a wispy, nonmaterial energy. She was fascinated by the radiant string and also horrified by it.

But her terror reached new heights when she watched her magic fly straight into the old man's hand and melt into his skin the same way Alaric's had. She collapsed, weak and drained, onto the snow beside her brother.

Their parents rushed toward them, but there was nothing they could do to help.
And within five seconds, the old man had drained Zaina, Cristiano, and Sage of their powers too.

All five siblings lost their powers to the old man. All five siblings dropped to their knees and let out groans of anguish as their parents held them close in their arms. For as long as they could remember, their powers had been with them, been a part of them.

Alaric with his ability to control the elements and talk to animals, Astraea with her magic and mind-reading, Zaina with her telekinesis and levitation, Sage with his super speed and strength, and Cristiano with his invisibility.

Like the very limbs attached to their bodies, their magical abilities had been a physical part of them. Having them all ripped away was like getting their hands severed off.

The old man chuckled to himself. "Excellent," he said, his voice like the purr of a cat. "Now I've made up for the purple diamond."

Alaric tried to rise, but he was too weak. Wincing, he stayed crouched on the icy cold ground with his brothers and sisters. He only had the strength to lift his head. And when he looked up, he found himself at eye level with the old man's wolf.

The white and silver creature looked the same as it did over a decade ago. But this time, Alaric didn't expect to make contact with him. His days of communicating with animals were long gone.

He was on the verge of hanging his head, breaking eye contact with the wolf, when he heard a voice echo in his head. It wasn't his own.

I'm sorry, Alaric, the voice said.

Alaric gasped. He recognized that voice—it was the gruff yet sweet voice of the wolf! *I can still hear you? But I thought he took all my powers!*

The wolf was completely still, but Alaric swore he saw him shake his head.

No, Alaric. Not all of them. You'll always have your love and kindness for animals.

Alaric couldn't believe what he was hearing. If he could still talk to the wolf, then maybe there was hope for him, hope for his whole family. He started to smile, then stopped himself. The old man couldn't find out about this—the only reason he had yet to kill any of them was because he was still under the impression that all the quintuplets were powerless.

"Well, I better get going," the old man said with a heavy sigh. "I have people to hypnotize, countries to take over, you know, what YOU were supposed to do, Alaric. Now that I've got all your powers, there's no stopping me from taking over the world! This entire planet may be completely different by tomorrow morning!" He flung his head back in a raucous laugh, then he reached down to grab the wolf's neck and shake him. "Hurry up, you runt! We're leaving!"

The wolf whimpered, his brown eyes pleading with Alaric.

Alaric gently spoke into his mind, *Listen, you've got to do it. You just have to. I know you can't imagine a life without him, but he's never really cared about you. You're just his slave. But I'll take care of you. I promise I will. But you have to do it... you have to kill him. You're the only one who can.*

Uncertainty flashed in the wolf's eyes. But then, slowly, it revolved on its paws and turned to face the old man.

Everything happened so fast. One minute, the wolf and the old man stood, facing each other. Then, in the next second, the wolf soared into the air, lunging straight at the old man. The force of the wolf knocked him down in a second; he cried out in pain and tried to push the wolf off.

But the wolf remembered that Alaric had promised to take care of him and remembered how Alaric had always been his friend in the old days.

With that in mind, the wolf felt no remorse as he shifted all his weight into his paws, pressing hard on the man's throat. Deep down, Alaric was a good person. The wolf couldn't allow him to be hurt like this. His one and only friend had to be avenged.

The wolf pressed harder, and pretty soon, the old man stopped writhing and choking beneath him.

Pretty soon, the wolf was standing on something hard and stiff and cold. The old man was dead.

And everyone was safe.

Chapter Ten
Happily, Ever After

Back in Zaina's cabin, everyone gathered in the living room to eat a second Christmas dinner—the same as the first but with Alaric and their parents added to the mix. Zaina felt horrible that their first dinner was ruined, that Theo had to cook all the dishes once again.

However, he assured her that it was no trouble since cooking was his passion.

Alaric sat on the floor in front of the fireplace, the plush rug cushioning him and the huge wolf he was petting. The old man had always arrogantly insulted the wolf, without giving him a proper name, so Alaric called him Silver.

Silver the Wolf lounged in front of the fire with his head resting on Alaric's knee. He snoozed in peace, thinking only of his new friend and not the corpse of his old master rotting away in Central Park.

Astraea walked into the room, having just gotten two slices of pie from the fridge. She hesitated at the doorway for a minute before striding towards the rug and plopping down next to Alaric and Silver.

"Hey," she said, handing him one of the plates in her hands. "You haven't eaten anything since we've been here. Have some pie."

"I can't."

"Come on, Alaric! You've been brooding like this for ages. Don't you like being with us?"

Astraea was joking, but Alaric's eyes clouded over.

"I just... I feel so guilty for everything I've done to you guys over the years," he said. "I don't know how I'll ever be able to make it up to you."

He murmured, speaking up only loud enough for his and Astraea's ears to hear. The others in the living room—Zaina and her family, Sage and his, Cristiano, and Darcy and Juniper—were all engaged in deep conversation. They were relishing a trip down memory lane, each of the siblings recounting parts of their childhood to the parents who never had the chance to be part of.

Darcy and Juniper, with beaming faces, listened to Zaina detailing her life with her wealthy adoptive parents—currently recalling the time she was given a pony for her ninth birthday! Everyone listened, nobody except Astraea paying attention to Alaric's concerns.

Astraea told him, "Look, Alaric. We've all made mistakes. But that doesn't matter. It's all in the past now. What you need to focus on is the here and now. None of us have any bad feelings toward you. We're just glad you've finally joined the family now!"

"Really?" At this, Alaric looked incredulous. His eyes widened onto Astraea's face, taking in her easygoing expression with shock.

She chuckled. "Well, duh. Come on, you're our brother. Even though sometimes we feared you, we always *wanted* you to be part of our lives. Just, you know, the good version of you."

Alaric actually smiled. Then, as the grin fought its way onto his face, he said, "I had no idea. I just thought I wasn't wanted anywhere, even with you guys."

"See, that's where you're wrong," Astraea said, holding up a finger. "Just because we weren't fans of the choices you made doesn't mean we didn't miss you and love you. Heck, I always admired you when I was a little girl! You were the cool one. The one who walked to the beat of his own drum."

"Yeah, and look where that got me." Alaric chuckled.

Astraea shrugged. "It took you on a journey to finding your true self, where you really belong. With us."

Alaric smiled at his sister, and she sent him a cheesy grin of her own in return.
Then he finally accepted the plate of lemon meringue pie and sank his teeth into a huge, delicious bite.

For a while, Alaric and Astraea sat in comfortable silence, eating their pies by the fire and listening to the hum of voices behind them. At the same time, the firelight played on their faces and surrounded them with warmth.

It wasn't until after the pie plates cleared and Alaric was back to peacefully stroking the wolf at his side that Astraea spoke again, bringing up something none of the quints had talked about yet.

"What about our powers?" she asked. "Aren't any of you sad about them being lost forever?"

It didn't take long after the gruesome death of the old man for all the siblings to realize that their magic had died with him. The wolf murdered his old master before there was ever any time to extract the power threads he'd stolen. Though the reality of being normal, powerless human beings crashed through their minds, none mentioned it.

Four days, three nights, and a plane ride had passed since that moment in Central Park. Yet, until now, neither Zaina, Cristiano, Sage, Astraea, or Alaric himself dared to bring up the sobering point.

But in the warm bubble they sat in together, the situation seemed like a safe one for Astraea to voice the deepest worries preying on her mind.

Alaric hesitated at first. His hand paused on the wolf's soft, furry body. "Well..." He thought about it for a minute before finally answering, "To be honest, I'm really not.

At first, it was kind of... *jarring.* You know, being without the very thing that made me who I am. But now I realize that my powers were just an ability—they weren't an entire person. There's so much more to me than just magic. Besides... it's kind of freeing, in a way. Now that I don't have so much power at my disposal, I can focus on living a normal life. Which, I think, is what I always truly wanted... What about you?"

Astraea nodded thoughtfully, secretly wishing she possessed some of Alaric's confidence. But she was still struggling.

"It's hard," she said. "My magic was my livelihood. All my income came from my nightly shows in Vegas since I was thirteen. I don't know what I'll do now to survive. No one will come to watch me perform if I can't do my infamous illusions anymore."

Alaric winced and patted her on the back. "I'm sorry. I didn't realize your powers were such an asset to you."

Astraea nodded grimly. But a minute later, she switched her expression to a smiling one and said, "But I'll get through it. Like you said, our powers don't make us who we are. We make us who we are. They were just a gift we had for a little while. I'll find a new job. Actually... I've always thought it would be fun to write a book. I always used to love writing when I was younger."

A huge smile spread across Alaric's face. "You'd be great at that, Astraea. You're the most creative out of all of us!"

"What are you guys talking about?" The intruding voice was Zaina's, and all of a sudden, she, Cristiano, and Sage plopped down on the floor beside Alaric and Astraea, joining their impromptu gathering and turning it into an official sibling meeting.

Astraea and Alaric looked at them in shock, then turned around. Darcy and Juniper were no longer in the room, and neither were Zaina's husband, Sage's wife, or the kids.

"Where is everyone?" Astraea asked.

"Apparently," Zaina said, squeezing in between Astraea and Sage, "Mom and Dad went to a toy store while we were still in New York and bought the kids a bunch of Christmas presents. Came as a total surprise. They're all in the next room, opening them, so don't be alarmed if you hear sudden shrieks every now and then. They'll be shrieks of excitement, of course."

"You know, this is the first time we've ever spent Christmas together, all of us in the same room," Astraea said.

Zaina gasped. "Oh my gosh, you're right! This really is the first time."

Alaric turned towards Zaina and smiled sheepishly at her. "Thanks for inviting me into your house, sis. I've always wanted to spend the holidays with family, and you just made that dream come true."

With a giggle, Zaina slung her arm around his shoulder, "Well, *you* made *my* dream come true too!"

"What was your dream?"

Zaina beamed at the four of them. "Having us all together like this, one happy family!"

Her eyes suddenly glistened with moisture; before she had a chance to let her tears fall, she blinked them away and changed the subject. "So, what were you guys talking about?"

"Our powers being gone," Astraea said matter-of-factly.

"Oh," Zaina's cheerful demeanor dropped at those words.

A slight tension pierced the warm atmosphere.

Alaric added, "We were just talking about how weird it would be to not have our abilities anymore. Astraea, especially, you know. She's got her whole magician thing going on. Now she won't be able to do it anymore."

"The same thing with me," Sage cut in. "I'm going to be a pretty lousy football coach without my speed and strength."

"And me," Cristiano added. "I'm the FBI's most valuable asset. Having the ability to become invisible and see into the future mean almost no organized crime escapes my notice. I'll surely lose my job now."

Astraea winced, then teased, "Looks like we're all going to be flipping burgers for a while."

"Oh, gosh." Sage rolled his eyes toward the ceiling and cackled, shaking his head.

"Sorry." Astraea shrugged. "I had to try lightening the mood. After all, it is Christmas."

"Guys, don't lose hope!" Alaric suddenly cried, snatching everyone's attention in an instant. As the other four siblings fixed their eyes on him, he continued, "You guys are powerful, even without your magical abilities.

Just think—it was your tenacity and bravery that made you capable of saving me. And if you were able to save even a lost cause like me, finding a career and living a fulfilled life should be a cinch for you. I'm not just saying that because we're family—you all are genuinely *awesome.*

Astraea, you're going to write an amazing book. Cristiano is going to continue on at the FBI because I guarantee you it was his wits and cleverness all along that kept him at that job. And Sage will go on being the most cheerful, uplifting, and caring football coach that ever existed. And who knows? Maybe Zaina and I will open an antique shop."

He looked around appreciatively at all the little trinkets Zaina had decorated the room with.

Zaina smiled. "An antique shop? How'd you know I've always wanted to open one of those?"

"Because of the way you decorate your house. It looks like something from the 16th Century." Alaric shrugged, then grinned at her. "Plus, we're related, and *I've* always loved antiques too."

The siblings watched Alaric with a newfound awe in their eyes, like seeing him for the first time.

Then Cristiano said, tentatively, "You really think I'll be able to stay at my job?"

Alaric rolled his eyes. "Come on! You're a ninja, even without the powers. But, of *course,* you will."

Cristiano turned fiery red as a genuine smile crept across his face. Pretty soon, everyone around the fire sported identical grins, grins of hope, love, and excitement for the future.

Alaric was right. This wasn't the end for any of them—it was merely the start of a new chapter.

Epilogue
Five Years Later

The teenage girl was shaking as she approached the table. Her eyes were wide and unblinking as if the woman waiting for her with a smile was a celebrity she couldn't bear to unglue her eyes from.

With red cheeks and trembling hands, the girl stopped at the table's edge and held out her worn and well-loved copy of Book 12 of *The Mystical Diamond* Series.

"H-Hi, Astraea," the young girl stammered. "I'm your biggest fan."

Astraea beamed up at the girl, who resembled her own thirteen-year-old, bookworm self in so many ways. "Aww, really? Thank you so much! Who should I make this out to?"

While she spoke, Astraea set the book on the table before her. She opened it to the front page, where the title, *Blizzard of Magic, The Mystical Diamond Series #12,* stood out in bold, mystical typeface.

"Uh, my name's Laura," the girl said. She leaned in closer, clutching the strap of her pink glitter backpack as she whispered, "There's a rumor going around that Alaric is based on someone in real life. Is he?"

Astraea started to smile, then pressed a finger to her mouth. "Shh! My lips are sealed."

The young fan's eyes flooded with admiration. She practically wasn't breathing the entire time Astraea signed her book.

"Oh my gosh, thank you! Thank you! I can't wait to add this to my collection!" Laura cheered in excitement.

"Thanks for all your support," Astraea said, giving the girl a hug (which immediately made her burst into tears) just before she left.

The next person in line was up.

Astraea was already giving the same one-liner she'd said a thousand times that morning, barely looking up as she reached for a different color marker.

"Hi! Who do I make this out to—"

Just then, she lifted her head and saw who the person at her table was.

Not one person, but *four.*

All of her siblings were there. Zaina, looking as beautiful as always. Alaric, a huge smile on his face. Cristiano, stoic as usual but also wearing a tiny grin. And Sage, beaming down at his sister with the same intensity her teenage fan had.

And all four of them were carrying copies of her latest book. Considering the entire series was inspired by them and based on the quints' real-life struggles and adventures, it was a huge honor and delight to see her favorite people holding her book. Astraea gave them each a teary-eyed smile.

"What are you guys doing here?" she cried happily.

"Are you kidding?" Zaina laughed. "Our bestselling author sister is having a book signing to celebrate her *twelfth* release. That's huge! How could we *not* show up?"

Astraea laughed off her flustered emotions and sent her sister a playful eye roll. "It's just a book! You act like I've landed on Mars or something. Besides, you guys should be the ones celebrating. Sage, I heard you led your team to victory at the last game, a true MVP."

With a cocky grin, Sage nodded. "Yes, it's true. It's really true."

The siblings all chuckled in unison, even Sage, amused at his own self.

Astraea's gaze shifted to Cristiano. "What about you, Cristiano? You're a little celebrity yourself."

Cristiano had recently done an interview on national news after using pure intelligence, hacking skills, and technological prowess to uncover the sinister plots of a group of terrorists and foil their plans just before they carried out their plan of attack on three of the nation's capitols.

Right now, the aftermath of what *almost* happened to America had everyone in a state of shock, awe, and admiration for Cristiano, making him even more popular than Astraea.

But the siblings would've never been able to tell by just looking at him. As always, he was dressed in a plain suit and wore an even plainer expression. He was not loud about his accomplishments, barely mentioning them at all. And when Astraea brought them up, he immediately blushed with a fiery shade of pink in his cheeks.

"Just a little interview," he said, shrugging.

Astraea scoffed. "Little interview, my butt! If it wasn't for you, I wouldn't even be having this book signing right now. This city was one of the targets they had in mind, remember?"

"Of course, I remember." Cristiano grimaced at the thought. "I guess you're right. I am *kind of* a hero."

Laughter burst out of each of their mouths, loud and unrestrained like giggles of children.

Finally, Astraea let her gaze hover over Alaric and Zaina's faces.

"What about you guys?" she asked. "How's the shop going?"

"It's going awesome!" Zaina responded. "Alaric and I have the best time, going shopping together, finding all kinds of ancient goodies to put in the shop. Just last weekend, we found this collection of old medicine bottles at an apothecary from the eighteen hundreds—with all the medicine still in them! It was so cool!"

"We can't seem to get new inventory fast enough," Alaric added. "At least a thousand people come into the shop every day. We run out of stuff too quickly!"

Astraea smiled so wide that her face started to hurt. "Guys, I'm so happy for you. *All* of you. I mean, look at you. Look at *us.* We were all so worried five years ago. We thought we'd never make it without our... our *gifts.* But now, look at all we've done. We're living the dream. And you know what the best part is?"

As if they all knew and agreed, intuitively, on that matter, all five of them shouted the answer at the same time, their synchronization like a perfect harmony.

"We're together," they echoed.

After sharing small, affectionate smiles, the four siblings each handed Astraea their copy of her book for her to sign.

A minute later, she finished the last book and handed it to Alaric.

"How about we all go out for dinner after I'm done here?" Astraea suggested. "We can call up Mom and Dad and have them join us too."

The quints were all in agreement that a happy family dinner was just what they needed after all the strange excitements that had been going on in their lives. So, they agreed to meet at an Italian place downtown, their absolute favorite restaurant, and then parted ways. Astraea held the hugest smile on her face for the rest of the book signing.

"To our lovely children!" Darcy exclaimed, holding up her wine glass so high that she almost knocked it into the golden chandelier glowing warmly over their table.

Juniper raised his own glass and added, "And to every single person in our wonderful family!"

The dozen people at the table raised their glasses and echoed, "To us!"

One by one, they took a sip. Sage, Cristiano, and Zaina's husband, Theo, had dark, rich ales; Astraea, her new boyfriend, Xander, and Sage's wife, Ria, had matching martinis; and Alaric and Zaina's glasses were filled with fizzy cherry coke, the same beverage the children at the table had ordered.

Resting between them on the long, oak table in the private room tucked away at the back of the restaurant was a feast fit for a royal family. All their favorite Italian dishes were fresh out of the kitchen, savory tendrils of steam rising into the air to tease their hungry stomachs.

Within seconds, nearly everyone at the table started digging in.

Zaina, Cristiano, Sage, Alaric, and Astraea picked up their forks. But before they joined the others, they peeked across the table at each other, meeting one another's eyes with faint, yet appreciative, smiles.

They all thought of the moments and experiences that had led them to this point, to the togetherness of this present time.

And as they took their first bites, grinning at each other, they all looked forward to the joys that waited for them ahead.

When you're with family, anything is possible.

Home is where the heart is.

POWERS UNLEASHED

THE MYSTICAL DIAMOND
Powers Unleashed